Into the Unknown

ISBN: 0-9856-6796-6
ISBN-13: 9780985667962

Into the Unknown

Book III:
The Survival Series

Travis Wright

"One, remember to look up at the stars and not down at your feet. Two, never give up work. Work gives you meaning and purpose and life is empty without it. Three, if you are lucky enough to find love, remember it is there and don't throw it away."
—Stephen Hawking

Prologue

The two ships stopped and hovered while they continued to try to contact the fleet.

"We have six incoming," Jim told Doug over the radio.

"I see them."

"Are you going to fire on them?" asked Captain Scott. "This ship does have weapons right?"

"We will only engage them if they fire first," said Doug. "They want to see what we are and they might get close enough for us to see them too, and yes we have weapons."

"I saw only a shell of a ship," said the captain. "What kind of weapons do you have?"

"Craig can you show the captain our complement please?" asked Doug as he pointed toward Craig.

"Over here sir," said Craig.

The captain got out of his chair and walked over to another console.

"Here are our ion pulse cannons," said Craig as he pointed them out on a display of the ship.

"Ion pulse cannons?" asked the captain.

"Yes," said Craig. "They're basically very advanced rail guns. The men in the suits have small versions of them too."

Jake opened his right forearm up and his cannon came out, then went back in. "They also have the same repulsion technology that the ships do. All bullets and missiles will just be pushed away," said Craig.

"You might want to take your seat captain," said Doug, "they're getting close."

The jets flew by and rolled away. The cameras onboard took pictures as they approached and got some good ones.

"They have North Korean markings on them," said Craig as he sent a picture over to the HUD for Doug and Captain Scott to see.

"They're coming back," said Jim.

This time the jets fired missiles at the ships. They of course had no effect and the ships opened fire with the ion cannons, destroying them.

Jim tried again to contact the fleet and again got no response. Anti-aircraft flak started to explode all around them as they got closer to the fleet, and they could see that a huge attack force of jets was inbound. The flak pushed them around the sky with each burst. It was all deflected, but the shock waves from the explosions hit them and made it a little more difficult to fly.

"Let's take care of these jets and then deal with the ships," Doug said to Jim.

"We're right beside you," said Jim. "I guess you could say that diplomacy has failed."

The two ships flew in to intercept and engage the incoming jets as the barrage of anti-aircraft flak continued to push them around.

The scene of the firefight in the sky must be spectacular from down below, thought Craig, as he continued to blow jets out of the sky with the ion pulse cannons.

"We have more inbound," Doug said to Jim.

"Let's go get em boys!" yelled Craig enthusiastically.

Chapter One: Domination

The ships flew into the mix of hundreds of aircraft as the anti-aircraft barrage cut into the enemy's own jets. The aero-dynamic, advanced craft had flown so fast that the gunners on the Navy ships below must not have anticipated their own jets moving in to attack at that point. They stopped firing from below once they realized they'd mistakenly hit their own, and it was only the jets shooting missiles and bullets at them now. The ion pulse cannons made quick work of the incoming aircraft. The gunners locked on each target and fired just as fast as they could. There were so many jets attacking the two crafts, that some of the missiles hit their own jets as they were deflected off course. This was acceptable to Jim and Doug as they continued to talk throughout the engagement.

Both of them had been fighter pilots in the Navy before joining NASA. They had seen combat in two separate conflicts in the Middle East. The fight in front of them was familiar and they knew what to do.

The two pilots made sure they kept their ships far enough away from each other to avoid any conflicts between them. The projectiles from each ship would be deflected as well if they happened to miss their intended target and this kept them safe too.

"I have six incoming on my starboard side," said Jim.

"Roger that," said Doug, "we have multiple bad guys at twelve, three and now ten o'clock."

The radio traffic between everyone onboard both ships sounded confusing, but all of the men were able to focus and listen to everything going on at the same time. A dogfight with so many aircraft should have been confusing, but this was what fighter pilots were trained to do.

Craig and Ray were the gunners on the ships and they coordinated their firing on a different channel simultaneously to avoid any possible confusion between them, the pilots and the navigators. They each listened to radio chatter in one ear and talked to one another in the other ear.

AJ was Jim's navigator. He was one of the newest people to get the gene therapy and had been a fighter pilot in the Air Force before the bombs fell. He and many others were becoming welcome assets in the collective.

"We need to get more information about why they were headed this way," said Captain Scott. "Can we land on one of the carriers and try to talk to them?"

"As soon as we take care of the rest of these hostile jets we can see how they feel about a boarding party," said Doug.

The jets kept coming at them, but less and less were approaching. They were either leaving the area, or being blown out of the sky. Both the Intrepidus and

Virtus were being tossed around the sky as missiles and the occasional anti-aircraft flak from below exploded around them.

"Can you contact your carrier sir?" Steve asked the captain as he walked in front of him.

"I can, but what would you like me to say?"

"They should land all of their jets and turn back," said Steve. "We can handle this situation and your resources are dwindling on that ship."

"You do have a point," said Captain Scott.

As the captain made contact with the Carl Vinson, Craig made an observation.

"The remaining jets are all breaking off, and so is the fleet," he said.

"Looks like it's time to land and make contact," said Doug.

"Intrepidus, this is the Virtus, over," said Doug.

"Go ahead Virtus," said Jim.

"We're headed for the flag ship to land and deploy suit soldiers and make contact," said Doug. "Can you cover us?"

"Roger that," said Jim.

The Virtus flew to intercept the massive aircraft carrier. As the ship approached, the carrier's defensive weapons opened up on them.

"We will have to take this barrage head on and let you boys get out quickly," Doug told Steve and Jake.

"We're ready when you are," said Steve.

The two men left the flight deck and walked to the back of the ship to the cargo bay. They waited for the go ahead before lowering the ramp.

The Virtus moved into position. It hovered above the flight deck of the carrier and lowered its ramp. The machine guns, which started firing on them as they approached, must have run out of ammunition. Either that or they realized that they had no effect like all of their other weapons when turned against the massive aircraft. This was a good time to deploy the soldiers. The two men in suits walked down the ramp and around the left side, only to be fired on by soldiers with automatic weapons. Steve and Jake opened up their shields and started to engage the enemy with the ion cannons that came out of their forearms.

The rest of the soldiers quickly retreated back into the ship as they saw what the huge mechanical things coming out of the ship were doing to their comrades.

Steve and Jake stood in front of the Virtus as Doug got on the loud speaker.

"We need to talk to your commander," he said in Korean.

Nothing happened, so Doug repeated himself.

A lone officer eventually walked out of the communications tower and started toward the ship.

"Doug, can you transfer the translation tool from the database to the HUDS in mine and Jakes suits?" asked Steve.

"On its way," said Doug.

The two men stood there in there suits absorbing the Korean language so they could talk to the man approaching them.

They finished just as the officer reached them, and Steve was able to greet him in Korean.

The officer was stunned and asked what they were.

"We are human," Steve replied.

"We're here to accept your unconditional surrender," said Jake.

"Can you speak for everyone in this fleet?" asked Steve.

The officer said that he was just a negotiator and that he would take their demands to his superiors.

Jake told him that they had ten minutes to surrender or they would be destroyed. Steve looked over at Jake who shrugged his shoulders. The officer walked back to the tower and left Steve and Jake standing by their ship.

The Intrepidus was hovering above them and monitoring everything that happened.

"How are the talks going?" Jim asked Doug.

"Steve and Jake have given the Korean officer our demand of surrender and are waiting to hear back from his superiors," said Doug.

As the two men were talking, a large strike force approached the Virtus from both sides of the ship opening fire with small arms and rockets. Steve and Jake opened their shields up to deflect the incoming rounds better and asked for instructions for engagement.

"I say they light 'em up," said Craig.

"I have to agree with him," said Jim over the net. "I'll drop two more suit soldiers in to help them."

"Roger that," said Doug.

The Intrepidus maneuvered alongside the Virtus and the ships ramp was lowered to allow two more men in suits to join Steve and Jake.

The four suited men deflected bullets and rockets while simultaneously firing their personal ion cannons back at their attackers. The two ships hovered and watched in support. They were being attacked as well, but didn't fire back because of the men they had on the flight deck. The whole engagement was recorded from the beginning on the digital recorders on both ships to be watched later for training purposes.

Other ships in the fleet were slowly maneuvering into position to possibly assist the carrier. The Intrepidus rose higher in the air and fired multiple shots at each ship on an intercept course. The cannons targeted aircraft on flight decks or communications platforms to show the ships the power they had. The ships slowly moved back out of the area after they were hit with the cannons.

The engagement only lasted a few minutes and left dozens of Korean soldiers dead or dying. Doug got on the ship's intercom and said that everyone aboard would be destroyed if hostilities continued.

A short time later, a short, older man with gray hair slowly walked out of the tower with half a dozen men walking behind him. He stopped in front of the suit soldiers. He saluted and bowed.

"I am Ro Han-Gyong, Supreme Commander of the peoples military. You have defeated us and we surrender," he said as he offered Jake his sidearm.

"You may keep your sidearm," said Jake.

"We have many questions," said Steve. "Why was your fleet on its way to the west coast of the United States? Why did you not answer the radio calls from the aircraft carrier or from our ships?"

"All good questions," said the commander. "I have many for you too, like what are you and what kind of ships are these? My negotiator said you are only human, so my best special forces unit took it upon themselves to attack."

Arrogance is radiating from this guy, thought Steve.

"You are in no position to ask anything," said Jake in a commanding voice. "Why was this fleet heading this way?"

"We wanted to finish what we started a few years ago," said the commander. "The might of the West was brought to its knees and we were coming to claim our prize."

"Can you believe the stones on this guy?" Jake asked Steve.

"Bring the commander aboard," said Doug over their secure radio. "I've heard enough."

"You need to head back to where you came from," Jake told the rest of the men from the carrier.

They just stared at the commander. Jake had to point his cannon at them and yell to get them to move away.

"Come with us," Steve told the commander.

At that point, the Korean officer was taken on board and put in a small room by the cargo bay after being disarmed. A few men from the strike team stood guard outside.

The ships rose above the flight deck of the super carrier and the ramps to the cargo bays were closed.

"I say we blow these boys out of the water," said Craig. "If they're really responsible for the destruction of our country then I say its payback time."

"It's not for us to decide," said Doug. We'll leave this in the hands of others. We have other things to worry about right now.

The ships gained altitude and started back to the Carl Vinson. The flight back was a low and slow one. The water was littered with debris of the aircraft that had been destroyed in the air. No survivors could be seen by the thermal imager.

"We have incoming," said Craig suddenly.

The ships turned in mid-air to meet head on the threat that was coming from their left flank.

Chapter Two: Annihilation

The fleet had turned back and was firing everything that it had at the ships. Large missiles with multiple warheads rocked the area around them.

"There are jets coming at us from the front and both flanks again," said Jim. "They must have had some waiting in reserve."

"Let's get some distance between us and the Carl Vinson," said Doug.

"It looks like they're trying to drive us back out to sea where the fleet is," said Steve, as he raised his visor and took a seat at a console.

"We need to stay together and attack en force," said Craig, who was busy engaging the jets and incoming missiles.

"I'm running low on two port guns," said Ray. "I'll need someone to reload them real soon."

"You shouldn't be out yet," said Jim, "check again."

The firefight was testing all the systems in the ships. They would be able to fix everything once it was all over and they were back home, as long as they survived.

Nothing had penetrated the hull in either ship, but they were being tossed around all over the sky again. They made their way toward the fleet as fast as they could in order to take out more of the threat.

"I'm hit," said Doug in the Intrepidus as a huge explosion rocked the ship. "I've lost two starboard thrusters."

"What the hell is going on?" yelled Jim. "That isn't supposed to be able to happen."

"I don't know, but we need to either end this soon or fall back."

"The fleet is getting into some sort of overlapping formation," said Steve as they approached it.

"We need to gain altitude," said Doug.

The ships flew up as fast as they could manage, but it wasn't fast enough. A few jets had been detected on an intercept course with both of them.

"They're coming in kamikaze," said Craig. "We have to take them out before they get too close."

Another jet hit the side of the Intrepidus and the ship started falling from the sky. The impact and resulting explosion ripped a gash in the hull this time.

"Virtus, we are going down," said Jim. "I say again, were going down."

"Commander, they have a massive hull breach on the lower levels in the berthing areas," said AJ, the navigator.

"Can you bring it back up?" Doug asked Jim.

He was fighting the controls with everything he had and a few hundred feet above the water, he finally regained control.

"Got it," said Jim.

"Was anyone hurt or lost?" asked Doug.

"No, with the small crew we have on board, most everyone is on the bridge at their stations," said Jim.

"Glad to hear it, can you stay in the fight?"

"We're on our way to inflict some damage now."

"Ray, ready the forward cannons," said Jim as the ship leveled back out. "We're going to turn the tides here."

The Intrepidus was just above the surface of the ocean and closing in on the fleet. The ion pulse cannons fired as fast as Ray could lock onto targets. Machine guns and missiles were redirected toward them and allowed the Virtus to focus on the last of the jets. Missiles shot up from below the surface and headed toward both ships.

"Craig, can you lock onto those submarines?" asked Doug.

"I can, but I don't know how much energy the projectiles will lose once they hit the water."

"Well, this'll be another learning experience for us," said Doug.

The Virtus locked onto the closest submarine and dove out of the sky toward it. Craig fired multiple rounds from the main cannon and they saw a large explosion from underwater.

"That answers that one," said Craig. "Let's go help the Intrepidus with the other ships."

The Virtus flew into the barrage of machine gun fire and anti-aircraft flack coming from the destroyers and other ships. The defensive weapons of the aircraft carriers also fired on them as they approached.

More and more ships began to sink, as the ion cannons continued to fire. Not many jets were left in the skies above, and the few remaining would be dealt with soon. Even after seeing that they had no real chance, the jets kept coming anyway.

The Intrepidus was still in the fight even with the damage to the hull and thrusters. The main engines and the rest of the thrusters were still working fine. Jim was a great pilot, even before getting the gene therapy. He was doing a fantastic job keeping the craft in the air.

"We just got hit again on the side with the hull breach," said Jim. "The repulsion has stopped working on that side of the ship. Virtus can you come along our port side and block all incoming ordinance from the breach?"

"On our way," said Doug.

Even with the commander of their fleet onboard the Virtus, the remaining crew down below must have figured that they had nothing to go back for. It seemed they had decided that dying in battle was better than anything else they had to look forward to if they couldn't reach the west. Many cultures regarded honor above all else, and a glorious death in battle was better than the shame of defeat.

The Intrepidus was limping around the sky, but continued inflicting massive damage on the ships still afloat. Doug took the Virtus back up and pursued the remaining jets. After being re-engaged, they were not taking any more prisoners.

No more aircraft could be seen on radar after a short amount of time, so the Virtus flew back below to help mop up the remaining ships. Craig took out two more submarines that were still firing on them as they descended on the remaining fleet.

Nothing fired from the ships that were still floating after a short time. They scanned the area for any further threats before they decided to leave again. The Intrepidus was in need of repair, but Jim was confident that it would make it back to the airstrip. They needed to drop off Captain Scott, so they proceeded to head back to the aircraft carrier one more time. The water had more debris in it now and some of the ships that hadn't sunk yet were on fire.

When they reached the friendly aircraft carrier, the flight deck was full of sailors and the few Marines that were left on board. The two craft landed side by side and as the ramps were lowered, the returning ships were surrounded by cheering people.

Jake brought out the Korean commander and handed him over to the sergeant at arms. The Marine grabbed the man, took the commander's sidearm from Jake, and looked at Captain Scott.

"He's your problem," Steve told the captain. "We have a different path to take."

"How can we get a hold of you if we need you again?" asked Scott.

"We'll be monitoring the area and will know if we're needed," said Steve.

The captain thanked all the people aboard the ships for their help and moved out of the way so they could leave.

The men all got back on board. Steve was standing on the ramp as they flew away. The ramp rose as he walked into the cargo bay. The two ships flew back toward the airstrip and home.

All the men and women on board the two ships were talking about the engagement on their way back. The idea that they had just defeated the people responsible for the destruction of life on the planet as they knew it was exciting and overwhelming at the same time.

The people back at the airstrip were given the heads up that the ships were on their way.

As the two ships flew in to land, they saw that they would be greeted by the entire compound.

After landing, the ramps were lowered and the suited soldiers and strike teams exited along with the crews. They were welcomed with cheers and applause from the population of the airstrip. Many of them had been listening to the engagement on the radio while they were gone.

The soldiers went to the armory to get out of their suits, and the strike teams helped them while they put their gear away. They went outside after everything was taken care of to meet their friends, families and loved ones.

There was excitement all around. Many were happy to hear that all of the hard work they had put into the ships was worthwhile. Some wondered if what was left of the United States military would become part of this group. Doug quickly told them otherwise.

"We are going down a different path than the people that stood before us," he said as he got up in front of the large group in the main hangar.

"What does that mean?" asked a man in the crowd.

"The things we're doing and building right now, on this land are for the future of mankind," said Ann as she stood up beside Doug. "You will all bear witness to what will become the future of humanity and be able to say that you helped make it happen."

Some of the people cheered, others were talking and looked confused. But the celebration that started after the return of the ships from battle went on for the rest of the night, with everyone in good spirits.

Chapter Three: Back to work

The work on the ships continued, and the crew that Jill had been working with while the others were away was doing a fantastic job. The fabricators were getting better with each new ship that they helped construct.

After the repairs were done to the Intrepidus, it was decided that more ion pulse cannons had to be added to all ships. The gunners on the ships would still have a job, but if the engagement became extreme, like it had against the fleet, the computers would have to take over on auto. The tracking, locking on and firing would be more efficient than even someone with advanced intelligence. The genetically enhanced abilities made them much better, but they were still only human. It was decided that the jet had not actually made contact with the ship, but it had detonated in such close proximity that the hull was breached. They had learned many things about the technology, the ships and themselves from the battle.

Material was beginning to pile up again, now that the first two ships were back to hauling it in. They were still meeting small amounts of resistance every time they went out for supplies. This was avoided as much as possible, but people were desperate and wanted whatever they could get a hold of. Once more people on the outside heard about the suit soldiers not being hurt by bullets, most people avoided the ships. This was a little disconcerting, since they were trying to help people too.

Life on the airstrip turned into a small community, and all of them enjoyed the life that they'd made. The newest people to join the group were glad to have so much after years of just making do, and sometimes fighting just to live another day. People always told stories about the hardships they had gone through after the nuclear devastation. Some people were just trying to survive and take care of their families and loved ones, while others were trying to control the fragile new world and everyone it it. This was always the story. Survival of the fittest and who had the biggest club.

"We're seeing more activity on the ground, but meeting less resistance as we go further into cities and outlying areas to get building material for the ships," Jim told the main group in their weekly meeting, one morning.

"Any idea what it means?" asked Chris.

"Not unless we stop and question people," said Doug.

"Maybe people are getting more desperate as time goes by," said Jill.

"We haven't encountered any planes or jets so far," said Jim, "but I think it's bound to happen."

"When can we expect completion of the next ship?" asked Ann.

"We're in the final stages now," said Jill. "We'll need more computer hardware and wiring, according to the technicians."

"I have an idea where we can find that," said James.

"Can you let me know when you plan on going out for the computer components?" asked Steve. "James and I need more material for the suits too."

"I will," said Jim.

"Can we spare a ship or some teams to monitor the situations in the more populated areas?" asked Ann.

"We might want to consider putting a ship into orbit to keep an eye on things or even a satellite," said Doug.

The others agreed that something should be done, and soon. No one wanted to be surprised by troops or aircraft and end up possibly killing the very people they wanted to protect.

They wrapped up the meeting and went on with their daily routines. Most days were pretty much the same. They rotated assignments to the various work details to mix things up. There had been no confrontations with the surrounding towns since the last attack, which had been dealt with decisively. The reaction teams and guard duty had been cut down to the bare minimum and the men and women were given new tasks to perform in order to speed up the projects' timelines.

Modern firearms were slowly being replaced by ion pulse cannons for most applications. They were more efficient than the encased projectile weapons and the user wouldn't need to carry all of the ammunition that they now did. Steve and James were still in charge of manufacturing the suits and weapons. Some of the newest people to join the community had expertise in the fields that the group still needed. The added help allowed them to put out more suits and weapons. They designed small hand-held cannons for the guards, which attached at the wrist, and larger ones for the hummers, just like they had built for the ships. Each ion pulse weapon that they made was able to fire well over ten thousand times before the core needed to be replaced. Karen had the idea of incorporating a gauge to show how low the core was. These started as dials and as the weapons were upgraded, they were all updated to digital displays. With a larger group now, better ideas were coming out of the whole that would benefit them all.

De Novo had stopped breast-feeding, so Karen was finally able to get the inoculation. She was excited and scared at the same time. She wanted to be able to contribute to the cause more and knew that this was the way to do it.

The day came when she was going to receive it, and she had a group of people there to support her. Most of the original group that had gone into the bunkers alongside her had gotten the therapy and were there in the room with her. Some of her other friends that couldn't get it at all stopped by to watch too.

Ann was going to give it to her, and had told her what to expect.

Just seconds after getting the inoculation, Karen felt as if all her senses had come alive, and worked better than ever. She was instantly aware of the changes that were happening to her. Her sight, hearing and sense of smell were all heightened even more than most of the men's. Ann explained to her that the females that had undergone the treatment all responded faster and better than any of the men did.

"Our genetic makeup, being able to reproduce and endure pain is the main reasons that we are smarter and can learn faster than the men. The only advantage they have is that they are stronger than us," said Ann, "just don't tell them we're smarter."

"I won't," said Karen smiling.

Twenty-four hour containment was standard now and she understood the protocol. Steve would take the day off to spend with the baby while this happened.

Ann was close to giving birth. Her baby boy was going to be the first human born that would have the genetic enhancements given to him by both parents, a development greatly anticipated by everyone in the compound.

Karen passed all the tests after her containment time and was ready to get to work. She knew where she could help out the most. She joined Steve and James in the fabrication of the suits and weapons. She brought many great ideas to the table before and after she received the gene therapy. She came up with how to attach different weaponry and add on accessories like jet packs and extra air tanks, making maneuverability in the suits much easier. These different attachments were designed to make the suit soldier's mission adaptable in a matter of minutes. They brought many ideas to the drawing board, but not all of them were implemented right away. They filed all of their collective ideas together, so they could possibly be built or used later.

Jill was the next to command a ship. As it was in the final construction phase, she would be receiving the latest and greatest that the builders, as Karen, Steve and James were now known, had to offer. Her call sign was Athena and she named her ship the Fortis, meaning valiant. She picked her crew and gave them their assigned places on the ship based on their expertise. Jill picked an all female crew based on their qualifications and was hailed as a visionary leader by all the other women that lived on the airstrip.

All the people that had been given the gene therapy had come up with call signs and ranks to make communicating while onboard their new ships and from one ship to another easier. Each pilot was given the title of commander of the vessel that they were in control of, while everyone else was a gunner, technician, navigator, and so on. Though each of them had the ability to do each others' jobs, they had their specialties. Craig was more than happy to stay in the gunner seat on Doug's ship and named himself Thor, the Norse god of thunder. Jim picked Helios, the sun god. The rest of the would-be ship commanders and crew picked out their call signs as well, each finding something that inspired them.

Six of the cruiser class ships were to be constructed. All of these ships would eventually be joined together to make one massive inter-galactic ship. More ships would be constructed after these six were done, but this was the priority for now.

Simon and Ann were currently working together on plant and animal hybrids. The research they were doing was based on the gene therapy they had taken, but on a smaller scale. Simon had the idea to create animals that were larger, both to produce more meat and also to live longer and produce more eggs or milk. His idea to make plants that would produce more fruit or vegetables was also very exciting. In a laboratory setting, they could alter cells and genes of anything to make them work the way they needed. If the experiments went well, they would be able to provide food for a much larger population, helping rebuild the planet. Food shortages had always been a problem around the globe before the war, and more than likely one of the causes of the disaster to begin with. With vast food supplies, there would be one less reason to fight; at least that was the hope.

The plans to rebuild the human race were slowly being implemented right there where the next evolution of humans had started.

Jill's ship, the Fortis, was now complete. The crew got onboard to go for their maiden voyage. The suit soldiers assigned to this ship were on board too. Ann wanted her whole crew onboard for every flight. After putting the ship through its paces on the ground, Commander Athena wanted to fly around the planet and visit places that had small civilizations. She wanted to reassure them that life would go on and that the golden age of man was still to come. Many people wanted to join the effort, but their main focus had to be on the population of the airstrip for the time being.

Karen, Steve and James were constructing a satellite cluster that would cover the entire planet and relay real-time information to a super computer also under construction by the group. It would eventually keep track of all things happening on the surface and beyond the planet. The ships would instantly get updates as well. Eventually anyone in a suit would be able to access everything available on the database.

A clean up of all the space junk in orbit was a priority before the satellites could be set in place. A group discussion would soon take place to determine the best way to do this.

As soon as Jill's ship was completed, they started on the next one. With the technology advancing almost daily within the group, they implemented new and better ways to make the construction faster and more stream lined. When something unique was added to the newest ship being built, the older ones were retrofitted so they were all the same. The airstrip and hangars were almost too small now for housing people, the ships and the construction all together. There was talk of leaving the area once a more suitable place was found. Many people liked the airstrip and the work that they were doing. They knew they were safe with the people and technology they were working with. Life outside the fence was brutal in so many ways.

More people were chosen to get the gene therapy, which only helped with the overall plans of the group. Ann still chose the people that would get the gift. "We can only have people that are true," she often said.

The group decided that a gigantic magnetic net would be the best way to get rid of all the space junk in orbit around the planet. Not all of it was made of metal, but the net should be able to collect most of it anyway. The plan was set in motion with the four ships that they now had. The net would need to be constructed and deployed in orbit with the four ships towing it to collect as much as they could. The net and all the material would then be set on a course to collide with the sun and burn up. After this was completed, the satellite cluster could be strategically deployed.

There was non-stop construction on the airstrip at any given time, from the ships, to weapons and more. More people joined the cause all the time, as more were needed for construction, and the airstrip seemed to be shrinking beneath the added population. The ship commanders were actively looking for a new place that would be suitable and able to accommodate all the people. They also needed space for the new ships that would be constructed in the future, as they made trips out of the area for supplies.

Steve had an idea to make small fighter versions of the advanced ships. Some questioned why they would need fighters when the cruisers had all the protection they would need, as well as weapons.

"If we needed a smaller recon vessel, we could just send in one of the fighters to do it, or we could use them as unmanned drones. They could be manned by a suit soldier and be just large enough for him or her," said Steve. "I'll make one and we can test it to see if we want to proceed with more."

The others agreed to this, and the team got started. Karen had the idea to allow the fighters to launch and land in a cargo bay. The bay would have to be retrofitted to have launch tubes and double as recovery platforms. With their enhanced senses and hand-eye coordination, the pilots would be able to maneuver and land in the tubes after their missions. If this was the direction that they wanted to go after the trials, then all future ships would be built to accommodate the fighters initially instead of being retrofitted later.

Chapter Four: Interdiction

An earth vessel in a low orbit was monitoring the old United States on a regular basis for awhile, until the satellite cluster was completed. While the new ships were being constructed, they were taking no chances of being attacked by anyone and they wanted to know what was going on around the globe.

Military commanders and government factions that had gone underground before the nuclear devastation were starting to resurface more now than they had before. Huge complexes like the one just outside of Washington, D.C. called Mt. Weather, had housed many so-called important people from the federal government. Some of these underground bunker complexes were essentially underground cities and could hold many hundreds if not thousands of people for a certain amount of time. They would eventually run out of supplies and need to resurface to either start over or replenish.

Small militias in many areas around the world had formed in the absence of law and order and taken control of communities that had started to rebuild, even soon after the bombs fell. These militias were slowly being eradicated by the military units in the old United States and other places mainly in small, but sometimes large skirmishes. The militaries had better weapons and vehicles as well as better trained personnel. More and more aircraft could now be seen in the skies in most parts of the planet as the ships flew around gathering materials. Life sometimes seemed to be getting better for some people, but the constant power struggles were taking their toll on all sides.

"We need to do something," Gary said as he was talking to Trevor in the medical building one day.

"Do something about what?" asked Trevor.

"I'm hearing more about the destruction and death going on out there all the time and with all the advanced technology we have...

"Stop right there," said Chris as he walked in on the conversation. "We have enough on our plates here. We don't have the time or man power to police the rest of the world."

"We can at least help out around the immediate area," said Gary.

"I understand your concern and we can talk about this as a group and decide on rules of engagement," said Chris. "But we need to focus on construction and taking care of who and what we have here."

"I agree wholeheartedly, "said Gary, "but we can't just sit by and watch the innocent die either."

While the guys were talking, Chris got a call on his radio.

"This is Chris, go ahead."

"Who are you talking to?" asked Trevor.

"He's on his radio," said Gary.

"Roger that," said Chris. "We might get attacked very soon. Get underground now," he said to the doctors.

They left the building and joined the others as they walked briskly through the hangar to the go to the established underground areas.

Somewhere in the skies above Montana, a couple of Air Force jets flew...

"Whisky Lima two six, this is Condor, over."

"This is Whisky Lima two six, go ahead Condor."

"There's quite a bit of activity in grid 6904 in the southwest quadrant."

"We'll fly over and have a look, anything specific we should be keeping an eye out for?

"We've had reports of strange ships flying around. Just need you to do a little recon and report back. Do not engage without authorization"

"Roger that Condor, Whisky Lima two six out."

The jets headed toward the airstrip. A confrontation had to be avoided if at all possible. The military jets were American and considered friendly. Doug had an idea and broke orbit in the Virtus.

"Where are we headed commander?" asked Craig as they flew down through the atmosphere. "I thought we had another day up here before being relieved?"

"We have to show ourselves to the AWACS and have them call off the fighters headed for our home. A fight with them must be avoided," said Doug.

The ship flew at top speed and soon caught up with the control aircraft. Doug moved alongside, matching its speed and then moving in front of it while flashing a bright searchlight in Morse code. The message read, "We come in peace and mean you no harm. Please call off your aircraft attack." They repeated the message and Doug soon received word from the airstrip that the fighters had altered their course. Doug flashed, "Thank you," with the light and then moved away and disappeared off the AWAC'S radar.

The radio communication traffic was going crazy, talking about the UFO that had contacted the AWACS in mid flight.

"That was incredible captain," said the co-pilot.

"Were we taping that?" asked the captain.

"We sure were sir," said the lieutenant.

"Communications," said the captain.

"Yes sir."

"Did those fighters divert like I requested?"

"They did sir."

"Where did that ship go?"

"We're not showing it anywhere on our scope," said the radar officer. "It's like it just vanished."

"How could they have maneuvered in front of us like that? We're going over five hundred miles an hour!" said another controller.

"What do you think it was?" the co-pilot asked the captain.

"I don't know, but whoever or whatever they were, knew Morse code. I sure would like to see what powers that bird."

The Virtus had accelerated and shot back up to maneuver into a low orbit. The crew was going wild. Doug's flying was amazing.

They had been in contact with the airstrip the whole time and were congratulated once they re-established orbit. The navigator could once again see the entire world down below.

"We'll have to make contact with the nearest military commander," Doug said to Chris on the ground.

"I agree, we don't want to start a war with our own people."

The Virtus would stay in orbit until it was relieved by the next ship. The group would discuss their options and where they would go to talk to a military unit commander. James suggested that they go see Captain Scott aboard the Carl Vinson. The others agreed they should try. The ship had been cruising up and down the California coast since they left it in the Pacific after the fight in the sky.

James tried to contact the ship, but got no response via radio. A strike team was assembled and Jill's ship, the Fortis, was taken with a delegation to go talk with the captain. They wanted to make sure that the military stayed clear of the airstrip and this might be a good way to accomplish that if the captain was still in contact with the rest of the military.

Doug, on board the Virtus, was in contact with Jill and her crew as they flew to make contact with the ship.

"We see nothing out of the ordinary from here," Doug told Jill.

"Thanks, let us know if you see anything that we might not have spotted as we approach."

"Will do," said Doug.

The Fortis was almost within viewing distance, and Jill had the hull shield pulled back so they could all see through the viewing window.

The Carl Vinson was drifting and no activity could be seen on the flight deck. They detected no aircraft in the area either. The Fortis hovered above the deck of the ship and the ramp came down. Two suit soldiers and a six-person strike team walked down it. As soon as they were clear, the ship went back to a high hover above the carrier to provide over-watch. The team made their way to the control tower. The suit soldiers had small cameras mounted internally on their helmets and sent a live feed back to the ship. A hatch was opened and a suit soldier went in first. The team made their way up the tower and secured operations. It was determined that the whole ship was on autopilot. They started a search of the vital areas of the ship to try and get some sort of an idea as to what was going on. They couldn't search the entire ship, which would take weeks or longer. The ship was massive and the team didn't want to take any more chances than they had to.

The team was re-called to the ship after less than an hour of searching and not finding anything that would help.

"We have incoming fighter jets," said Jill to the strike team. "You need to get back here now."

The ship was soon taking off from the flight deck of the carrier, moving at great speed just above the water to avoid radar. After they reached land again, the ship climbed. They flew right by the jets and could see the American markings on them.

"Doug, did you see where the jets originated from?" asked Jill.

"Yes, they came from a base in the Mojave Desert."

"Well then we must go visit them. Jim will be up there to relieve you in the Intrepidus very soon."

"Roger that," said Doug.

They tried to figure out why there was no one on board the aircraft carrier. Doug mentioned that with very few supplies, maybe the crew abandoned the ship to go back to land. Since all the ports on the west coast had been destroyed, they had nowhere to dock the carrier.

The Fortis and her crew flew back to the airstrip to continue helping with the construction of ships, weapons and other projects.

A ship continued to stay in geosynchronous orbit to keep an eye on the airstrip and the surrounding area.

A plan was put together to visit the base in the desert soon.

No activity out of the ordinary could be detected in the area around the airstrip as the Intrepidus sat in orbit.

"When will those satellites be done?" complained Ray.

"They will be done soon," said Jim, a little annoyed. "Have you finished the diagnostics on the pulse cannons?"

"I have," said Ray. "I know you don't want to hear any complaining, but this weightlessness and silence is unbearable."

Jim and Ray were on the night watch of the skeleton crew. They all knew that what they were doing was just temporary, but it didn't mean that they liked it.

"Go close the hatch to the bridge," said Jim.

Ray unbuckled from his chair and pushed off. He floated over to the hatch and pushed the button on the wall. The door closed and Ray pushed off the wall. He floated over to Jim's chair and grabbed a console to stop.

"Okay, it's closed, now what?"

"Close your eyes," said Jim.

"I don't know you that well," joked Ray.

Ray closed his eyes after Jim glared at him. Ray heard a guitar and opened his eyes.

"Is that..." started Ray.

"It is," said Jim as it got louder.

Sweet Home Alabama by Lynyrd Skynyrd was playing very loud on the speakers and both men smiled.

They floated around the bridge and played air guitars and drums as the song continued.

As soon as the music stopped, Ray looked over at Jim. "Is that the only song you have?" he asked.

"No, there's a whole library here on the ships computer, that's just one of my favorite ones."

"I like that one too," said Ray, "but can we find something that isn't fifty years old? And why did you have me close the hatch?"

"So we didn't wake anybody else," said Jim. "Go ahead and pick out a playlist to help pass the time."

Ray had forgotten that all the different rooms on the ship were soundproof, as all the walls were steel. Jim's idea had made the night pass quickly and before they knew it, the hatch was opening and the rest of the lights turned on in the room. Jim turned off the music as soon as this happened.

"What the hell is going on here boys?" asked Ben as he floated into the room. "Did I hear music or was I just imagining that?"

"The silence was getting to Ray," said Jim. "Was I the only one that knew that there was music on the drives?"

"I guess you were," said Ben as he sat down. "Did anything important happen while we were sleeping?"

"All's quiet up here," said Ray with a smile.

The men left the bridge to go and get something to eat and get some rest.

Chapter Five: Time and Space

Steve had been spending a lot of time outside at night just laying out on the tarmac and staring up into the night sky. He was very focused during the day working on projects, but after dinner, he would disappear. Karen was concerned, but Ann reassured her that whatever he was doing would soon be revealed.

Karen wondered how Ann could know that and what she meant by it, but didn't ask. After almost two weeks of staring at the night sky, Steve stopped suddenly. Karen was glad to have him back and so was De Novo. A few normal days passed, then Steve started spending his nights in a small hangar. Karen couldn't handle it any longer and went to see what he was doing.

"Honey, can I talk to you?" asked Karen as she walked into the hangar.

"Give me just a minute," said Steve. "I'm almost done with this part here."

Karen stood there watching him work on something that she couldn't make heads or tails of. She knew he would let her know if it was important or if he even wanted her to know what it was.

The two of them talked for awhile and Karen expressed her concerns regarding the way he had been acting. Steve told her how he had felt so compelled to watch the night sky and to make the device that he had been working on.

Steve was making a strange device that looked like a lamp. Even he didn't understand why he was making it. He had designed and helped develop many things since getting the gene therapy, things that had helped the whole population on the airstrip. He had worked on this new project in his spare time, but it was starting to cause problems at home. Karen asked if he needed any help, but he told her that he had to make it on his own.

The days and nights passed very quickly and then one night Steve asked a select few in the group to join him in the hangar where he had been spending so much time. They gathered together and Steve started manipulating the device that he had made.

When he was done, he flipped a switch and a very bright and blinding light emitted from the device. A holographic image appeared. It was like a large version of a human, but looked strange. It had two arms and legs, but only three fingers and a thumb. Its head was large for its body too. A voice spoke from it, but no one could understand what it said. It sounded like someone talking from underwater. Steve turned a knob slowly and it was suddenly speaking English. It sounded like it was a recording. They all listened intently to the message and seemed very happy and then sad toward the end. The recording had been sent specifically for the people listening.

A dying alien race had been projecting their thoughts into the minds of a select few humans on

Earth for years. They'd sent them across the great expanse of space in order to pass on their knowledge. They knew their fate and hoped that the humans would learn from their mistakes and be able to overcome the genetic problems that they had faced for thousands of years. The aliens had learned how to fix the genetic issue that plagued their race, but it was too late for them to reverse it. They wanted to pass on their knowledge to the closest beings in the galaxy that were a near match to their genetic makeup and their intelligence. They were skeptical at first because of all the anger and violence that humans had shown, but saw promise in them as well. With the slight enhancements that Ann and the others had made to the human genome, they now had the ability to bring their race out of the dark ages and into a new era.

It was agreed among the small group that what they had just learned would have to be kept from the rest of the population at least until the rest of the ships were completed. The select few would keep the secret until they thought it was the right time to tell the rest of those who had received the gene therapy.

Karen now understood why Steve had been acting so strangely even before the bombs had fallen and destroyed so much of the planet. The way that he knew what to do and where to go had been a mystery but nothing about their survival and where they all were now was a coincidence.

Little had been revealed about the race of humanoids from so far away except that they were dying, and they had a gift to give. Many of the humans wondered how old the message was and whether the aliens were still alive. These were questions that some wanted answered. The reasons that the interstellar ships were being constructed now made sense, but some wondered if there was a particular destination in mind. Time would tell, and as Ann often said, "All will be revealed."

Construction continued on the next ship. Ann was to command this one, but some wondered if she should wait until sometime after her baby was born to take on the responsibility. She said that she would be ready to take on both tasks. Doug fully supported her and so did many others. Karen had offered to watch the boy while she went on missions or just for the work day.

Soon after her ship's construction started, Ann was ready to deliver her boy. Gary and Trevor had never seen any woman deliver a baby so fast and with such pain resistance as she did. An hour after delivering him, Ann was up on her feet and walking around the medical building showing her new born off. With more and better equipment in the medical building now, the doctors were able to do so much more for their patients than they had before. If they couldn't find what they needed, they made the machines.

Ann named her son Postremo, meaning future. Everyone understood why she did it, but the name was considered a little odd by some. Most ended up calling him P or Mo. The boy's advanced intelligence was immediately apparent. He was very alert right away.

Ann was back at work the following day to help build her ship. Karen watched Postremo as she had offered. DeNovo was interacting well with the new baby and this made Karen very happy. The two boys were the youngest members of the community that lived on the airstrip.

Karen was glad to take the time to spend with the babies, but knew her help was needed in the making of suits, gear and weapons. She went looking for Ray to see if he could make a play pen for the boys so she could help out more. She found him in the common area downstairs. He was sitting in a recliner moaning when she walked up.

"What are you doing Ray?" Karen asked as she approached him.

He didn't answer her, and rocked back and forth. She could see the headphones in his ears now, so she pulled one out and he opened his eyes and sat up.

"What's going on Karen?"

"What are you doing in this chair?" she asked with a strange look on her face.

"It's a shiatsu massage chair," said Ray smiling. "I know I don't need it, never get sore muscles anymore, but I still like a massage and I can't seem to find a real masseuse."

"I see," said Karen. "Ray I was wondering if you could build my little guy and a friend a playpen so I can continue to work."

"I would be glad to. Does it need to be one cell or two? Just kidding Karen, I will start in the morning if that's okay."

"That would be great, thank you very much."

A few days later, she was back at work with the boys right next to her.

The Fortis was in orbit watching the airstrip and the rest of the United States while the others continued work on more ships and other projects. Jill was on duty on the bridge one morning when the computer started saying "proximity alert" She floated over to the center console to look at the radar and saw what the computer was talking about. Something was fast approaching their position from outside the solar system. She sounded the alarm for general quarters and, within a minute, the crew had taken their stations on the bridge. The object was headed right at the ship. Sara, the weapons officer had a lock on the object with the starboard pulse cannons in no time, and asked for permission to fire. Jill gave the go ahead and Sara fired a volley.

"I don't know what it was, commander, but it's gone now," said Sara.

The navigator had activated a few cameras and was just starting to bring the video up on the HUD when Jill asked her if she had hit anything.

"Stop and magnify that," said Jill as the crew watched intently.

The video recording was stopped and magnified.

"Is that a ship?" asked Samantha.

"It looks too small to be a ship," said Jill. "Sara, was it completely destroyed?"

"It appears to have been vaporized. I didn't pick up even small pieces after I fired."

"I want to widen the scans," said Jill. "We need to know what it was."

The crew got to work on trying to find the object or at least some part of it.

Meanwhile down below, Samantha picked up movement outside the city. There were vehicles on the highway moving toward the road block across the river from the power plant. This was a concern, and had to be investigated.

Jill contacted the compound about the convoy inbound for the city. Craig put the airstrip on lockdown and assembled a strike team to investigate. By the time the team had reached the main gate, the convoy was approaching. Craig got out of the lead Hummer and ran over to the gate. He waved his arms and the vehicles stopped. A man got out and yelled over to him.

"Why are you stopping us here?" asked the man.

"Minefield," yelled Craig, as he pointed in front of him. "What can we do for you soldier?"

"We're here to investigate what is going on here on this airstrip," said the man.

"I can't let you through," said Craig.

"We're here on behalf of the President of the United States," said the soldier. "You are hereby ordered..."

"Listen here mister," bellowed Craig. "I am Colonel Craig Jackson, United States Marine Corps and this base is under my command. I have authority under..."

"I'm General Christopher Hoyt, Colonel, and again I order you to open these gates."

"General, my orders in this top secret compound supersede your rank. Now unless you can bring me the President and have him order me personally, well buddy you're just plain out of luck. If you don't leave immediately, my men will open fire on you. You have three minutes starting now," said Craig as he looked at his watch.

With that, Craig started walking back to the Hummer. After he got in, the vehicles on the other side all turned around and left. They drove into the city and stayed there. Jill was asked to continue to monitor the situation for the time being.

Construction continued, but the completed ships were kept in the hangar until they could figure out what the military unit was up too.

The satellite cluster was almost done and Steve was very happy with how they turned out. The incorporated repulsion technology into the satellites as well as defensive ion pulse weapons would help their longevity. The onboard computer would be able to maneuver out of the way of meteorites, too if they couldn't be destroyed before they entered the atmosphere.

After much discussion about the men that had wanted access to the airstrip, Craig and Jake decided that they would go into town and do a little recon. They left after dark the night following the arrival of the soldiers in the vehicles. As they encountered people on their way into the city, they asked if anyone knew why the soldiers were there or what they wanted. Not many people would even talk and if they did, it was that they knew nothing.

"Why are they so scared?" Jake asked.

"That's another question that I'd like answered," said Craig. "But many people left the city once the new leadership from across the river took over."

The two men entered a tall building in the city center and used their enhanced hearing and vision from the roof to seek out anything that might help them.

"I think I have something," said Craig after some time.

"What is it?" asked Jake.

"There are two soldiers coming down the street talking about not wanting to be here, and how they wish they were back on base. Let's go and talk to them."

The men ran down the stairs to the bottom of the building as fast and as quietly as they could. Once on the bottom level, they made their way to the front of the building to intercept the men.

"They're separating," said Jake as he got close to the windows.

Craig was already making his way toward the man left on the street. Jake went out to assist him.

They surprised the soldier and quickly took him into the building they had just been in. They found a small side room off the lobby and they took him in for an interrogation.

"Why are you and the rest of the soldiers here?" asked Craig.

The man was very forth-coming and very scared. Craig wondered if he had been tortured before.

"We came here to get information about what's going on out on the airstrip," said the soldier. "That's all I know."

"What do they think is going on?" asked Jake.

"I told you I don't know," said the soldier.

"We can either do this the easy way or the hard way," said Craig. "It's your choice."

"Okay, but this is it. I heard some of the officers talking about alien spacecraft. There was a recent encounter by an AWACS and they think it has something to do with the airstrip."

They thanked him, and Jake put his arm around the man's throat. He choked him until he was unconscious so he couldn't raise the alarm before they got back to the airstrip. If they could avoid a confrontation, they would.

Craig and Jake left and made their way back to the compound to tell the others what they had found out.

The next day, Jill alerted the airstrip that an unmanned drone was orbiting above the compound. It was most likely taking either video or pictures. Craig walked outside with a sniper rifle and downed the small aircraft with one shot. This made it clear that there was still an occasional need for encased projectile weapons. It fell to the earth inside the fence. Jake took a small team out to retrieve it. There wasn't much left of it, but Steve and James said they would try to recover anything of importance.

Onboard the Fortis, Samantha was running a diagnostic on the sensors when she came across some information about the object that they had detected earlier, the one they'd thought destroyed a few days before.

"It's where?" asked Jill when Samantha told her.

Apparently when Sara fired on the object, it wasn't destroyed. It was knocked off course and impacted on the moon.

"Do you know where it landed?" asked Jill.

"I do," said Samantha. "I'm sending you the coordinates now."

"Good work. Unfortunately, we'll have to wait until another ship can either relieve us or go retrieve it themselves. Until the problem with the soldiers on the ground can be resolved, we're stuck here."

The information about the object was relayed to the compound and preparations were made to retrieve it when they were able.

Jill continued to let the people on the ground know about the aircraft and troop movements they were seeing. She wanted to get back down there to help the defenseless people of her struggling planet. She could see they were being wronged by military, militia and gangs. The lawlessness needed to stop.

Sitting idly by without being able to replenish the dwindling supply of raw materials that were needed to continue construction was beginning to wear on many in the group.

If they wanted to continue their construction plans, they needed to reach out and either form an alliance or put the fear of God into the people that wouldn't leave them alone.

They developed a plan to reach out to what was left of the United States military in order to come to an understanding with them.

Chapter Six: The Base

As they approached the remote desert base, a voice on the radio began to issue a message. "Unidentified aircraft you are in restricted airspace. Unidentified aircraft proceed on heading 201 out of the area or you will be considered hostile and you will be fired upon."

"Commander, should we respond?" asked AJ.

"No, just keep heading toward the airfield."

An F16 buzzed by the ships and the radio kept repeating the same warnings. They crossed into the base, came to a sudden stop and hovered over the airfield. They were approached by four AH-64 Apache attack helicopters while troops in Hummers and tanks approached on the ground.

Commander Helios finally answered on the radio. "We mean you no harm."

"This is General Nathan Wallace. What are your intentions?" the voice on the radio answered back.

"We wish to talk to you and mean you no harm," said Helios.

"Why did you ignore our calls to leave our airspace? This is considered an act of war. You need to leave now."

"We only came to talk to you," said Helios.

Seconds later, the Apaches and ground troops all opened up on the ships, but their weapons had no effect. Bullets were redirected and missiles veered off course and exploded. After a short volley of fire the military group realized that the ships were deflecting everything fired at them. One of the helicopters was hit with redirected ordinance and fell to earth, exploding on impact.

Commander Helios radioed to the general to cease fire.

"You can plainly see, general, that you are no match for us. Please lay down your weapons and call off all aircraft, or we will be forced to use our weapons."

The response was what they thought it would be. The area around the ships lit up again with fire from all sides. More aircraft were being hit by re-directed ordinance, which was now hitting troops on the ground as well.

"Fire the main weapon at the far left building as a demonstration," said Helios.

A loud, high pitched sound and bright light shot out from the lead ship and destroyed the hangar.

"This is your last warning," said Commander Helios over the radio.

With that they heard a cease fire called from General Wallace. The remaining aircraft moved out of the area. The tanks and remaining ground troops and vehicles stayed where they were.

"We will accept a delegation to discuss what you would like from us," said the general.

The Virtus landed while the other ship continued to hover. The loading ramp was lowered and six suit soldiers walked out to meet the general, or so they thought. As they walked down the ramp, machine gun fire erupted in their direction. They opened their arm shields to deflect more bullets. The men in front of them began to fall from the bullets ricocheting back toward them. The soldiers didn't even need to open up their pulse cannons from their arms.

"Cease fire!" came a loud voice.

They moved forward still deflecting the bullets being fired at them. Finally the shooting slowed and then stopped as soldiers lay dead or dying on the ground.

"This is not what we wanted!" yelled Helios, his voice radiating from the ship's intercom.

A soldier ran toward Joe with a bayonet on his rifle, but Joe grabbed it from him. The rifle broke in his hands like a twig. He picked the soldier up off his feet. "Do you want to die boy?" he asked.

His legs dangling, he squeaked, "No!"

Joe put him down, towering above him by almost 3 feet. The titanium suits were very menacing to look at. They were much taller than the soldiers were.

"Listen to me," said Commander Helios as he walked down the ramp. "We want to harm no one. You brought this all on yourselves," he said pointing at the destruction. "All we wanted was to talk to you, now you are going to give us this base."

A tall man with a cigar in his mouth walked out of a close building with more soldiers surrounding him.

He asked who or what they were and what they wanted with the base.

Commander Helios addressed the general. "We want your base. You have 24 hours to comply. If you do not leave or try to reinforce, we will destroy all of you."

"Why do you want our base?" asked the general.

"That is not your concern," said Helios.

"Are you human?" asked General Wallace.

Commander Helios raised his visor, stared down at him and said in his commanding voice. "We are human and so much more. We are superior to you in every way. Do not try our patience." With that they all walked back up the ramp and left the area with more speed than the soldiers had ever seen.

The damage to parts of the base was extensive. Broken up aircraft were in pieces and burning. Mangled soldiers were lying all over the place. The general was standing there in disbelief on the tarmac.

"What do we do sir?" asked a soldier.

"What can we do?" said the general as he walked back into the building.

Jill and her crew had been up in orbit for a week longer than expected and were all getting restless.

"What does it look like down there?" Jim asked as they flew away from the base.

"They're tending to the dead and wounded right now," said Jill. "I'll let you know when or if they start to leave."

"Roger that," said Jim.

Diplomacy had failed without even having a chance to start. The soldiers attacked without provocation and that in itself was their undoing.

The original plan was to go out to the base that housed the unknown aircraft and soldiers and talk to them. By attacking the ships, they made diplomacy far more difficult.

Jim had made a command decision to demand control of the base once they opened fire. A base in the middle of the desert would be a nice installation to use and defend. There would be much more room for the ships to be stored too. They hadn't decided yet if they would move the whole facility from the old airstrip, or keep the manufacturing plant where it was and run missions out of the desert base.

In the meantime, Doug took the Intrepidus up with his crew to relieve Jill and the Fortis. They had tried to keep the ships a secret for as long as possible, but could do it no longer. Construction of more of them would continue, helping them to bring stability to the planet.

The Intrepidus established an orbit next to the Fortis, and Jill sent over the latest updates they had via a wireless connection. The Fortis broke orbit once Doug had all the information. They were headed for the moon to try to recover the object that had been heading toward them a week before. Four suit soldiers were in one of the cargo bays awaiting touchdown before going out to find the object. Since they had made first contact with it, Jill said that her crew would be the ones to examine it.

Jill brought the ship down a few hundred meters away from the coordinates that Samantha had given her. The ramp was lowered once the bay was de-pressurized. The soldiers walked out and started toward the coordinates with caution. Their helmet cameras sent back real-time video to the ship, as well as down to earth for the others to see. The women walked to the top of a fresh crater and looked down upon what looked like a small ship. As they got closer, they could see that it looked more like a missile, or bomb.

"Any advice here?" asked one of the soldiers as she scanned the object.

"See if there are any buttons, levers or separate sections," said Steve after a few seconds.

"I see nothing on the side that is above the surface, and it's not emitting any heat or radiation that I can tell," said the soldier. "Wait," she said. "I am getting some interference on the AM bandwidth. Jill, are you picking up any radio waves?"

"Yes, very faint," confirmed Jill.

"I think it might be a probe," said James. "Can you get it into the cargo bay and bring it down here?"

"I don't think we want to bring it down here until we know more about it," said Chris.

"I agree," said Ann, "We should send up a team with more equipment and work on figuring it out on the moon's surface. Jill, come on home."

The suit soldiers made their way back to the Fortis. Once on board, the bay was re-pressurized and the ship made its way back to Earth.

Doug and the crew on the Intrepidus were seeing quite a bit of activity at the base in the Mojave. Jim onboard the Virtus was asked to head over to monitor the situation from a closer distance.

"They're defiantly leaving," confirmed Jim as he flew in closer.

As soon as what appeared to be the last vehicle leaving the base was out of the area, the ship flew in low and slow over the entire base, scanning for life signs and anything out of the ordinary.

"It all looks good from here," said Jim over the radio, as he landed the ship by the main cluster of buildings.

Suit soldiers deployed to recon the area. They all made similar reports as they walked around the base. It looked like the occupants had all left in a hurry.

"Jim, I just picked up four high altitude bombers headed for that base," said Doug. "Looks like if they can't have it, neither can we. I recommend that you and your men get airborne. I will break orbit and try to intercept them."

Suit soldiers ran back from all areas of the base once they heard the call about the possible bombardment.

Doug flew the Intrepidus down through the atmosphere as quickly as he could, without risking burn-

ing up in it. As he came down, he could see the bombers in front of him. He leveled the ship out as he saw
them and matched their altitude and speed. He then
moved in front of them and carefully nosed up to the
lead bomber. He could see the pilot and co-pilot right
in front of him. The ship was just a few meters in front
of the bomber. Doug could see the terror on their faces
as he got on the radio to warn them to veer off course or
be blown out of the sky.

"Attention Air Force bombers in front of my
ship," began Doug. "Leave this area now or you will be
destroyed."

"Whoever or whatever you are, you need to get
out of our way," said a voice on the radio.

"I will not warn you again," said Doug. "Leave
your current heading now, or you will die."

With that, Doug flew the Intrepidus up and over
the bombers, coming in behind them. He was hoping
the threat would make them leave, but so far it didn't.

"Doug, you have two fighter jets coming up behind you going supersonic," said Jim, as he entered the
area.

"I see them on radar," said Doug. "I would rather
not shoot any of these bombers down, but they won't
listen to reason."

"Why don't we just shoot their wings and they'll
have to bail out," said Craig, "that way were not killing
anyone."

"Sounds good to me," said Doug. "Go ahead Thor,
take one out."

Craig got a lock on the wing of the far right bomber and fired. The wing was cut in half by the pulse cannon. The massive jet started to spin out of control and lost altitude fast. Only five parachutes were seen opening up. They hoped that all of them got out, but couldn't know for sure. The remaining bombers continued on toward the base and the fighter jets started firing missiles at the Intrepidus. The bombers deployed flares, the only defensive things they had.

Jim moved in behind them and Ray shot the wings off of the fighter jets, hoping to avoid setting off any ordinance. They fell from the sky without any explosions and parachutes could be seen popping open. Doug moved into position above one of the bombers and landed on top of it. Using his thrusters, he forced the jet down until its engines cut out. He could see men bailing out of that one too. There was a few more this time. The last two bombers banked left and moved out of the area.

"Mission accomplished," said Doug on the radio.

"That was interesting, to say the least," said Jim.

"Let's get back home and check on the satellites."

"I'll get back up into orbit for now," said Doug.

"Thanks for the assist," said Jim.

"Anytime brother, we'll see you soon."

The two ships went their separate ways, while a search party from the military was looking for men in the desert below with helicopters. The Intrepidus planned to monitor the situation for awhile longer.

The soldiers that had come to the airstrip and were poking around town had left after the last encounters with the ships. The former cities of Clarkston and Lewiston were now under the protection of suit soldiers and the advanced technology. A few people had to be dealt with that were keeping the cities in a state of fear and panic. An ion pulse generator was installed on the grounds of the power plant by the river and tied into the power grid so that they had more and cleaner energy. The walls that were started by the inhabitants of the city were completed with the help of the ships and more people from the airstrip. The minefield around the airstrip was taken back out and disposed of. The people of the cities came freely to help with construction, and with all the new plants and animals food distribution also started to get back on track.

Chapter Seven: Helping Others

The situation on the ground had stabilized for a short time and most were glad for it. No one wanted to harm the American military, but would not have them showing up and telling them what to do either. Like it or not, this was not the world they all used to know. Laws and enforcement of them no longer applied. Survival of the fittest and strongest was the new law. The people on the airstrip were not bad people, but they would protect what they had and protect the innocent as well.

A few months had gone by since the last incident, which allowed for construction and planning to help others.

Jill was spearheading the efforts with her ship to reach out and help the communities of people that were struggling to survive. She had been working with Simon and Ann whenever she could.

The satellite cluster was finally complete, but before it could be put into place the space junk had to be cleaned up. The Fortis and Intrepidus would be going up to try out the net and hopefully get it all taken care of. With more to worry about on the ground and with Ann's ship not yet complete, the net was modified to be used by just two ships. It may take longer to accomplish the mission, but they weren't going to leave anything unprotected even for a short time.

The crews on both ships were ready to go up and deploy the magnetic net to capture the space junk in orbit around the planet. Steve and his group had adapted jet packs with thrusters for the suit soldiers going up. They would exit through the cargo bays of both ships and hook the net between them. This would allow the ships to fly at slow speeds to capture as much as possible. Once the net was full, they would slingshot everything toward the sun to get burned up. The gravitational pull along with the velocity of it should help it all get there. Something like this had never been attempted and no one knew if it would even work. Jim would go up in the Virtus to watch from a distance and give support if it was needed. He and his crew would be able to monitor the ground and the ships in front of them simultaneously.

When all three ships were in place, the suit soldiers were sent out of the cargo bays to hook up the net. Hooks had been placed on the outer hull of both for attaching the net. Four people had gone out in suits to do this and accomplished it very quickly. Once they were back inside, the net was activated and the ships started to move forward. They used the onboard computers to navigate through the field and capture items. All was going according to the plan until a very large piece came floating at them at great speed. It could impact the net and either fly through it, or cause the two ships to collide. Either way, it had to be stopped. Craig locked on as soon as he realized the potential problem, and fired a pulse cannon. The old rocket booster was blown into thousands of small pieces, most of it gathered up by the net. The rest of the mission went very well. Once the net was full, it was time to move toward the sun. Both ships attained an ideal matched speed. Once they were far enough away from the earth's gravitational pull, and reached a fast speed, they reversed the polarity on the net and both ships hit full reverse on their thrusters. The net emptied toward the sun instantly and they were ready for round two. After a few trips, the scopes on the ships' radars were virtually empty and the satellite cluster was deployed around the planet. With three ships putting the satellites into their positions, it went fairly fast. Once activated, they would align themselves to cover the entire globe, and be able to see anything in the air, on the ground or at sea in real time.

The ships were no longer needed in orbit to keep an eye on things below. The three ships flew back down to earth and to the airstrip. They could watch their hard work on the monitors in the computer room that had been set up. Once linked, the ships and eventually the suits would have access to the information on the mainframe.

As the satellites came online, a 3D image of the planet appeared above the center screen in the middle of the room. The surrounding screens showed the overlapping imagery from each of the satellites. Many things could be accessed now that they were up and running. Nothing on the planet could hide from the sensors. With the speed of the ships and the planetary monitoring, they would be able to go to anyone's aid very quickly whenever needed.

With all of the ships and crews back together on the airstrip, construction was once again at full capacity. Ann's ship was near completion and many other projects were getting done fast. The move to the desert base was slowly beginning to take place after perimeter security was installed. They all decided that the completed ships and their crews would stay in the desert and construction would continue on the airstrip for the time being. Shutting down the plants and moving everything would take vital time away from the well oiled manufacturing machine they had going.

Once the plant and animal hybrids that Simon and Ann had been working on were perfected, an effort to reach others on the outside was put into action. This was a coordinated effort with each ship commander and their crews. Volunteers eagerly went along for the humanitarian missions as long as it didn't interfere with any project they were working on.

Most small communities and pockets of people were just trying to survive. The militias and military units that were warring were bringing the conflicts to the civilians, most of the time unintentionally. The innocent and bystanders needed protection and food. More people would be needed to make these efforts successful. The small communities that were starting to benefit from the crew's efforts had very few people. The earth's human population had dropped to a near extinction level compared to what it had been before the devastation rocked the planet just a few short years before.

After the satellite cluster was operational, they made a semi accurate count of the remaining humans left on the planet. According to the information that the computer collected from satellite imagery, there were just over three million people left worldwide. Many parts of the globe were still uninhabitable after the nuclear fallout, even after years, and could continue to be so for a very long time. Every area would be closely monitored. There could still be people hiding deep underground, and there was no way to tell when they might resurface.

Back on the airstrip, the fifth ship was ready for construction. Ann's ship the Fides, meaning reliance, was now done and sent on a mission. That mission was kept secret from most of the others. Anyone that knew anything wasn't talking about it. The other cruiser-class ships had all been redeployed over to the desert base to run missions from there. The community was now divided, but many knew this day would come and were okay with it. Families were kept together, and friends were able to visit one another when time allowed for it. Doug turned over command of the Virtus to Steve for use on the airstrip and would command ship number five when it was completed. He was now overseeing the construction of his new ship and couldn't command the Virtus, which had been the first ship constructed. It would stay with the inhabitants of the airstrip-turned-factory for whatever they needed it for.

Ann's son Postremo was crawling after just a few months and was already starting to form words. It was anticipated that he would be walking soon too. Gary and Trevor made it a point to have Ann bring him in for regular checkups and his progress was well documented. With a large portion of their people at the new base, more construction workers could move onto the airstrip. Most of them were glad to be a part of something again and also happy that they didn't have to struggle to survive. The addition of new people caused problems from time to time, but the issues were dealt with accordingly and life went on.

Small skirmishes between military units and sometimes civilians were detected. Ships were sent out to these areas and the conflicts were stopped by the suit soldiers. People all over the planet talked about the advanced ships and suit soldiers. Allie picked up radio signals from time to time and she would tell everyone about what she heard.

With the help of the invincible people, as the suit soldiers were now being called, the people on the outside would have what they needed. Before they could planting gardens or growing new animals on the new base and in other communities, they would need a barrier to protect them from the outside threats.

They constructed high walls around each community and integrated repulsion technology into them. Auto pulse cannons were mounted in towers all around the perimeter as defensive weapons only. They built an impenetrable structure in the center of each compound that housed an ion pulse generator and a super computer to run everything. No one would be able to get in without access privileges and the people on the inside the walls would be able to live in peace. Anyone in the communities now under the protection of the invincibles that dared to cause problems, commit crimes or resort to any kind lawlessness at all would be cast out, never to return.

The original idea was to have the inhabitants of the communities that accepted the soldiers' help build most of the structures themselves. However, in many areas, there were not enough people. Help from surrounding communities were sometimes enlisted to help. This was usually a good option. It allowed people to reach out and find lost loved ones or friends once thought perished.

Many places around the world were being transformed by these new people that came to help. Most were glad for the aid; others didn't like giving up their freedom and being stuck behind walls. No one was forced to stay, and if they wanted to leave they could. The old world had failed miserably in many ways, and the new one that the people now looked forward to emerged in new ways daily.

The technology that the suit soldiers brought with them couldn't be handed over to just anyone. That kind of power in the wrong person's hands could inflict massive destruction, which was demonstrated by the events that led up to the world's current predicament.

As more ships were constructed and more people enlisted to help, more of the planets remaining population was protected by the invincible people and their technology. The community barriers were enlarged in some areas, to allow for population expansion. Eventually life spans would be longer and health would be better for all inhabitants. Disease was soon to be a bad memory in mankind's history. Not all humans would be able to get the gene therapy, but they would all enjoy living healthier. Other modifications to the genome were discovered and allowed for the other people to live healthier and more productive lives.

Once communities fell under the protection of the super humans, as they were also called, they were asked to help out in the construction of certain items that would speed the re-construction of the planet.

More secure locations were now available for these construction purposes. If life on the planet was to go on and thrive, then the advancements that were now available would have to be used. Only certain parts of the whole engine or formula would be built in each area. Only the original people that received the gene therapy could be trusted until a better way to regulate the technology could be put into place. A combined global effort was the end goal, with everyone working together to achieve the same result.

Within a short time, most resistance from military and militia groups had ceased. They finally realized that their weapons were no match for the advanced ships and suit soldiers. The old phrase, "if you can't beat them, join them," began to take on a whole new meaning. Taking over the planet and bending it to their will was not the goal of the invincible people, peace and tranquility was. They wanted to hurt no one, and with everything at their disposal now, this could all be avoided.

"Can you believe everything that's happened in the past few years?" Nancy asked Karen one day as they were eating in the main hangar.

"It's truly amazing isn't it?" Karen replied.

"We've all been so busy with everything, that I don't remember the last conversation like this with any of my old friends."

"We will always be friends," said Karen.

"What are you wonderful ladies talking about?" asked Gary as he sat down next to Nancy.

"We were just reminiscing," said Nancy. "This has all been a fast and interesting ride since our past lives in Billings."

"It has hasn't it," commented Gary. "I have to say that despite all the bad things that have happened to all of us and our friends, we have prospered pretty well."

"It would be nice to have all of them still with us," said Karen.

The happy mood of the conversation shifted as they thought about their friends and family that more than likely didn't survive.

Steve had gone out with a few other people in the Virtus when they weren't too busy, to search for friends and relatives that might still be among the survivors on the planet. They didn't tell anyone outside of the small crew that had gone out searching. They didn't want to get anyone's hopes up. All of the people that now resided inside one of their barriers anywhere on the planet had been documented and put into a database along with any new person seeking safe haven. Not all the people on his list could be found, but from time to time he would bring back a lost loved one for an emotional reunion.

After just a few weeks, Steve and his crew found Maria's mom living in what used to be Mexico. She had been on vacation when the attack happened and was just barely surviving when the crew found her. When the ship landed at the small mountain village and the suit soldiers walked down the ramp, the people thought aliens had landed. Steve quickly reassured them that they were not. They were surprised when he asked for

Maria's mother by name and showed him where she was right away.

When Maria was asked to meet the ship upon its return, she was confused until her mom walked down the ramp with the aid of two men. She was screaming as she ran up the ramp to meet her. It was the home-coming that Steve and the rest had hoped for. Some of the volunteers had enlisted to help, hoping to find loved ones too. Even after having no luck, some of them continued on with the endeavor to help others. They found Kim's sister and some of the other original group's family members and friends as well. Steve never found his brother or any part of his family. But many people were reunited by the effort of the Virtus and the crew. Some people that had been stranded on the other side of the country or even the planet found their way home with the help of the invincibles.

Chapter Eight: The Probe

The object that Jill and her crew aboard the Fortis detected while in orbit some time ago had not been forgotten. It was finally time to go and investigate it, now that everything had calmed down and a mission could be put together. Two ships, the Fortis and the Intrepedus, would take their crews and many others with expertise in useful areas to the moon. They'd go with many types of equipment to try to figure out what the object was.

Steve and James were modifying a few instruments the morning of the mission. When Jill's crew initially landed and inspected the object, they didn't see a way into it. Before opening it, they had to see inside to make sure that it wouldn't explode or release anything harmful, that's why they left it in the crater.

The ships were ready and everyone going was on board.

"Fortis, this is the Intrepidus, over," said Doug.

"Go ahead Intrepidus," said Jill.

"Just checking our coms Athena."

"I hear you loud and clear commander. Let's get this show on the road."

With that, the two ships rose out of the desert and shot up through the atmosphere. The trip would take them just a few hours and any final preparations could be made en route.

Down on the desert base and airstrip, more people were joining the cause. Many had qualifications in areas that needed filling, but most were just hungry and wanted help. Everyone would be able to help out, either with construction of something on the bases, or in one of the communities around the country. More and more people with military backgrounds were showing up at the gates of communities under the protection of the invincible people. Craig was in charge of security checks. ID badges were issued to all new people and they were told that they couldn't be without them. The badges had transmitters in them so everyone could be accounted for at all times.

The transition to using security badges on the airstrip wasn't well liked for many of the occupants. Most opposed them and said that they had lived there for many months or longer without them and had no problems. It was explained to them that the badges were for their safety so everyone could be accounted for.

The ships were closing in on their targeted coordinates on the moon. Every precaution would be taken in order to ensure that everyone would be kept safe. After landing, only the suit soldiers would be going out onto the surface. Many of the others wanted to, but not all of them had suits. Most were just glad to have been in space and many expressed how great it was to have the chance to be involved with the project, and be on the moon. What they were all doing was something that they never could have imagined.

With the gravity on the moon, all aboard the ship would be able to move about just as freely as they could on Earth. This of course made everything move smoothly. Once they gathered all their gear, ten suit soldiers walked and rode toward the object. Two special rovers had been constructed to hoist the object out of the crater and move it out to level ground so they could inspect it. X-rays were taken and other devices were used to try to determine what it was. Only half of the object was visible, so they carefully excavated around it in order to put straps on it. The cranes were put to the test as they hoisted the thing out of the crater and put it on a rover. The object was extremely heavy and the rover's tires dug into the lunar surface. The second rover had to pull the loaded one out of the crater with tow straps. Once on the flat ground by the ships, more tests could be run. The crew leaders decided that everything would be done outside, just as a precaution.

A large work area was set up and lights from the ships turned on to aid the soldiers. The object was lowered onto the hefty table they had made with cradles, based on the initial pictures they had from the previous mission. All of the instruments that they had used trying to see inside or get a material composition had been useless. They tried a saw with a diamond blade on one end, with no luck. After breaking three blades, they knew they had to try something else. A plasma cutting torch had no effect either. There seemed to be no way inside. The team decided to retire for the night to try to come up with something that might work.

The video feeds were live and the people on the airstrip and on the desert base that had been watching were working on a way to get inside too. One person suggested liquid nitrogen, using it to freeze the object so a piece could be broken off and tested. Another suggested a high intensity laser to cut through.

Allie overheard some people talking about the object and she suggested music. She was told to leave the hard stuff to the adults. She walked away with a sad look on her face and went up to the communications tower. She turned on the radio and started turning the knobs for someone to talk to.

The next day, on the moon, the crews tried many more things on the object and they still couldn't get into it. The liquid nitrogen looked as if it froze the end of the capsule, but it wouldn't break off. The laser idea was a bust too. The laser just reflected off and one of the soldiers caught part of it. The laser cut through part of his suit before he knew what was happening. The laser was shut down and he was rushed aboard the nearest ship.

"This isn't going well up here," said Steve on the radio. "Are we out of ideas?"

"One of the kids mentioned music down here last night," said Jake. "It was discounted and she was shut down for bringing it up, but we might as well try it, nothing else is working."

"I think she meant harmonics," said James. "Was it Allie that brought it up?"

"It may have been. I wasn't in the room, I just heard about it."

"Can you find her and put her on the com?"

"I'll find her now," said Jake.

While they were waiting for Allie to get on the radio, all of the other equipment was moved out of the way.

"Doug," said James on the radio.

"Go ahead."

"Can you get ready to play music on the outside speakers?"

"Roger that, but why?" he asked.

"We might have something that will work finally. I'll let you know when were ready and what to play."

"James, I have Allie here," said Jake.

"Hi Allie, how are you doing down there?"

"Pretty good, what do you need?"

"Jake was telling us that you mentioned using music last night to open this thing up here."

"I did, but the adults all told me to go away," said Allie.

"I'm sorry they treated you like that, I will talk to them when I get back. What exactly did you mean when you said we should use music?"

"Well, not music really, but different tones," she said. "I was just guessing since you haven't been able to open it with anything else."

"Thank you Allie," said James. "I will let you know if it works."

"Doug, can you play a small part of all the music you have on the onboard computer and see if anything happens?"

"Starting now," said Doug.

A few hours went by and nothing happened

"Try breaking down individual notes," said Steve.

The computer broke the music down and played everything separately.

"This will take time," said Doug. "All of you might as well come back inside and relax while we do this."

"Roger that," said a few of the soldiers. They walked back up the ramps into the cargo bays of their ships.

Doug continued playing everything he could think of. Meanwhile, video cameras watched from three different angels. The computer continued throughout the night and into the early morning hours. Finally, everyone was woken up when the news came in that there was movement from the object.

The crews of both ships went to the observation decks. Doug, on the bridge of the Intrepidus, stopped the tunes from playing until the soldiers could get into their suits and get outside.

Steve was the first to get out to the table. The others were right behind him.

"Doug, can you play the tune that made it move?" asked Steve.

"Here we go," said Doug.

It was a simple piano tune and the object started to vibrate until other music joined in, then it stopped.

"Go ahead and stop Doug," said James, as he walked over. "Can you play each piano note separately?"

"I'll bring it up and start it in a minute."

While they were waiting for Doug to find a program in the computer that he could do this with, they stood there talking amongst themselves.

"What're you thinking James?" asked Steve.

"I think it may just be a combination of individual sounds that will open this thing up."

"Whatever it is, I think we're close."

Doug told everyone that he was ready and started going through each piano note, recording the ones that had any effect. In all, twenty-three different sounds had some kind of an effect on the object.

"I want you to isolate those sounds and try them in combinations one at a time please," said James.

"That's a lot of different combinations," said Jill on the radio.

"More than a billion to be exact," said Steve. "Maybe we should go back inside, this could take awhile."

Just as they were all walking inside, Doug said, "Hold on everyone, it's moving."

"Play that one again," said James, "the one that made it move."

Doug played it again and the object's shape started to transform, and then went back to its original shape.

"Play it over and over," said Steve.

Doug did as he was asked and the object continued to transform until it looked like an antenna. They walked over to it, and suddenly all the power in the suits and the ships went out. The computers on the ships started running through all of their memory very fast, a process the people aboard couldn't stop from happening. The whole event was displayed on the HUD and monitors. The suit HUD's were doing the same thing. Everyone scrambled to try to figure out what was going on, and then it all went black again.

The object transformed back into the shape that it started out as, and then shot into out into space fast, breaking the straps and part of the cradle. There was nothing anyone could do; all the electronics were down. Without any warning, everything came back to life, lights, computers and communications too.

"What just happened?" someone asked.

"I think we were just scanned by something very intelligent, and gave it all of our information," said Doug.

"Can you tell where it went?" asked James.

"Not a clue," said Doug. "With nothing on when it left, it couldn't be tracked."

The people on the ships and on the lunar surface were standing there wondering what just happened, when Jill had an idea.

She brought up the feed from the nearest satellite and magnified the video. The whole event played on the HUD of her ship. She sent it over for Doug to watch too. They all saw the two ships on the surface of the moon, the lights going out and the object leaving the surface and heading back out past Mars.

"Well there you go," said Jill. "It got what it wanted and left. Nothing we could do against that advanced technology."

"I believe it was testing us and our level of intelligence too," said Steve, "the question is why now?"

The soldiers packed everything up and re-boarded the ships. All the time and effort they had put into the mission had afforded them no results, and they had probably compromised themselves and the planet. There was no way to know exactly what had just happened, but they were not going to take any chances.

Chapter Nine: Fortification

Group leaders decided right away that if the life forms that had sent the probe wanted to attack, considering the level of technology that the people on Earth had at the moment, they would not be ready. Early warning systems would have to be put into place and more powerful weapons would have to be designed just in case. They already knew that the ion pulse cannons had no effect on the material the probe was made of. Every precaution would be taken to ensure the survival of human kind.

Steve was in charge of designing an early warning satellite that would be positioned in amongst the asteroid belt making up the outermost ring of Saturn. The thought was that by putting it there, it could remain hidden. Many different types of sensors would be incorporated into it, along with cameras and video feeds that could identify anything on the elliptical plane of the solar system. They would transmit that information back to Earth.

James and Karen started looking into making a weapon that fired multiple projectiles at the same spot for maximum penetration. They went through the database and found a weapon that was futuristic in its design in the early 1990s. The company was developing stacked projectile weapons systems that fired in succession. This might be the answer they were looking for. The probe had been knocked off its course by the ion pulse cannons. Four rounds were fired at the object as it approached the Fortis and they didn't know how many projectiles actually made contact with it. Nothing they had used to try and get it open on the lunar surface worked. The probe was made of some kind of material not found on Earth. Once done with the weapon design, they would need to test it. If it proved formidable, they would make weapon platforms to be put in strategic areas surrounding the planet and beyond.

"We know how to make the weapon," said James, "but what kind of material should be fired from it?"

"I think Ben is tackling that issue right now," said Karen.

"It would be nice to have either the probe still available for testing, or at least some of the material."

"I agree," said Karen, "but I hope we never have to go up against an enemy that has ships or armor made of what the probe was."

They got back to work and knew that it wouldn't be long before they had a working prototype.

Another group of people in the design and construction area of the compound which Ben headed up were tasked with making a material that was stronger than anything currently manmade. Different materials with the properties they needed were combined together on cellular levels and tested for penetration. The people in the group studied the data base available to them and spoke with engineers and workers on the construction crews to try to achieve the best results.

Construction of the next ship continued on schedule and the work tempo slowly increased. Not knowing what may be heading their way made things worse. If leaving it all behind was the last resort, they had to be ready to do so.

Was the probe a threat? Was it from another civilization far away that was just curious? These and other questions were on many of their minds. Capsules had been launched into space from Earth on a few occasions in the twentieth and twenty-first centuries, containing a massive amount of information about Earth and every language and culture. Humans had actually invited anything or anyone else in the galaxy to come for a visit. This was of course a major controversy before the capsules had been launched. They could inadvertently be inviting an invading army to their doorstep too.

Ann was back and working day and night on getting her ship ready for its next mission. Doug understood her willingness to get it ready to join the others, but reminded her that she needed to spend some time with Postremo too. The child was walking and talking before he was a year old. He was the most advanced child anyone had ever known. Just like all children, he was a sponge, soaking up everything around him, but much faster. He could recite entire conversations back to people that he had overheard the day before. They all knew that he would become a major asset to their cause.

"Was the last mission you went out on a success?" Doug asked Ann.

"We'll soon find out," she said.

Doug knew what she had taken her ship and crew out to do; he was just trying to make conversation with her. She had a lot going on and was focusing on doing the best she could. While pregnant with Postremo, she had not been able to contribute as much as she would have liked and was trying to make up for it.

An idea was brought to the group about looking beyond Earth for materials to aid in the defense technology. Ann and her crew aboard the Fides had already been going to other planets to get samples. This was a bit of a shock for the others to find out, but most understood the reasons for secrecy. They had found a material on Mars that could prove to be the strongest and lightest material ever found or made. Samples had been brought back and tested.

A comet would come through the solar system any day and this was to be Ann's next mission. When her ship was leaving Mars on their last outing, the ship's sensors detected the distortion in space. Set on the highest magnification and resolution, the ship's cameras were able to get pictures and the sensors picked up direction of travel and speed.

The comet was not one that had been in the system before, that they knew of. It could have originated from anywhere. The mission was to land on the massive piece of rock, take geological samples, and land on the nearest moon surrounding Jupiter to run tests.

James and Karen had completed a prototype weapon that they hoped would be able to thwart an attack from anywhere or anything.

Ben and his team put together a barrier of hybrid titanium alloy that they had been working on, among other things, to be used as a target. The sample that Ann and her crew brought back from Mars was looking promising, but still needed more time before it was ready.

The test was to be conducted in the Mojave Desert just outside of the base that had been commandeered some time back.

Cameras and sensors were set up to monitor the test. The stacked projectile weapon was mounted on the Virtus for stability and access to the internal power supply of the ship. If the weapon proved viable, it would be retrofitted on the ships anyway.

Everyone was aboard the ship and the observation windows were open.

"We're ready to commence the test if you think your material can take it," said James to Ben.

"We are green across the board," said Karen, "if you boys can rein in your testosterone."

"I didn't even get a chance to fire any insults back," said Ben with a smile. "Yes, we can proceed when you're ready."

"The first test will be with our current ion pulse cannon complement," said James. "Craig, you can fire when you're locked on."

"I've been waiting for you ladies to stop jacking your jaws," said Craig.

James stared at him, so he turned around in his chair.

"Firing one round now," said Craig.

The main cannon fired from the front of the ship with a loud, scream-like sound. The projectile impacted within a split second of firing. Dust kicked up upon impact and they had to wait until it settled before they were able to see anything.

The video cleared up and the picture was displayed on the HUD for everyone to see.

"I see slight burn marks," said James as he inspected the video.

"There are no apparent fractures or penetrations," said Karen.

Ben's team was semi cheering at this point.

"Were not done yet," said Craig. "Permission to fire," he asked.

"Commence when ready," said James.

Craig was firing before James was done with "commence."

The ion cannon fired a large volley right at the center of the target. The hits were grouped very close together and some on top of one another. Once Craig was done, the dust had to settle again. It took a little longer than before, with all the rounds fired.

The dust cleared and the target looked charred.

"Scanning with thermal, x-ray and infrared," said Karen. "I still see no penetrations or fractures," she said after a few minutes.

The people on the ship were very excited and cheering very loudly.

"Okay, calm down everyone," said James. "We still have the final test to run. Craig, again you can fire when ready."

The new weapon fired as it was designed to. A long volley of two dozen rounds fired into the target. It looked like only one round was fired, because they all followed each other.

A shockwave followed the last round as it impacted the target, and more dust than was caused by any other impact flew into the air. They all waited in anticipation of the results.

When the dust had settled this time, and the sensors scanned the area, there were groans from the crowd. The video showed a hole in the center of the material.

"What do you think Karen?" asked Ben.

"We need to inspect the target physically, but from what I can tell the projectiles didn't penetrate all the way through. In fact from what I can tell at this point, they sealed the hole that they had started. The massive build up of heat brought the surface temperature up so high, that it started to melt the projectiles and the target itself."

"So if I had kept firing, it would just make it seal back up completely?" asked Craig.

"Very possibly," said James, "unless we could get some high explosive rounds thrown in the mix. A detonation might just have a catastrophic effect."

"Well, at least we know that this new material is stronger than what we currently have on our ships and suits," said Ben. "We should seriously consider retrofitting the outer hull of each ship and re-plating the suits with this."

"We might want to hold off," said James. "We have Ann taking samples of the comet soon and the material sample from the Martian surface still needs to be evaluated."

The target and all the equipment were collected, and they all went back to the base to continue working.

The Fides was approaching the coordinates of the comet's trajectory. The onboard sensors picked it up very quickly and a plan was set in motion to approach it from the rear. The tail and debris that followed would have to be carefully negotiated. All viewing windows were closed and the auto pulse cannons were ready. To avoid hull penetrations, Ann would have to concentrate on finding the best route in to land on the surface. The auto cannons would destroy any debris on a collision course with the ship as they flew in.

The comet was made up of many types of metals that the sensors could recognize, but some they couldn't. These were the ones they were after.

The closer the ship got, the bumpier the ride was. For safety reasons, there were just enough people on-board to fly the ship and run the equipment on the surface. They all had suits on with jet packs and extra oxygen tanks. If the ship was hit or had to be abandoned, they had to be able to survive out in space while a rescue was attempted. For this reason, locator beacons had been installed in all of their suits.

"We're three thousand kilometers away and closing commander," said the navigator.

"Roger that," said Ann.

The auto cannons were doing a great job as Ann brought the ship in closer. The comet was six miles wide at its widest area and almost eighteen miles long. It would have a small amount of gravity.

Once they got within a few hundred kilometers, the debris cloud covering the tail slowly disappeared and they could see the surface clearly. The ride became a smooth one and the auto cannons came to a halt.

"Find me a nice place to land," Ann said to the computer.

The heads up display screen in front of the crew showed the comet's surface and lit up the places that had material deposits, and their sizes. They figured the optimal place to land was next to the largest deposit of foreign material.

The ship came in slowly and the thrusters brought it down matching the speed of the comet hurtling through space.

After the cargo bay was de-pressurized they lowered the ramp. The soldiers brought the equipment out onto the surface of the comet and commenced drilling to obtain core samples.

Chapter Ten: Resistance

As if it wasn't bad enough that an outside threat possibly existed, the realization that the people that were accepting the group's help were capable of turning on them was even worse.

The addition of prior military personnel from the old United States into the new communities that were now flourishing was welcome for the most part, but in some ways an issue. People that were used to getting their way and telling people what to do would cause internal problems sometimes.

Prior politicians were continually trying to worm their way back into positions of power in some communities, yet everyone was expected to help out in all areas. Working together for the collective on every issue or task was a hard thing for some to come to terms with. There was no longer money to buy anything with; bartering for necessities was the way things operated now. If a person didn't have anything to trade, then they worked for what they needed or wanted.

There were some that had a problem with the new ways and wanted to bring back the old ones.

A small underground movement by those handy prior military types was starting according to the radio chatter that satellites had been picking up.

"What do you think we should do with this intel?" Chris asked Jim when they found out.

"We should monitor the situation and hope that they come to their senses. We've brought most of these people back from the brink of death by starvation, relieved them of fearing the person next to them. Each of these areas we have helped rebuild now have stability, food, electricity and are safe from those that would hurt them. What more could they want?"

"We do need to tighten up on security around vital areas," said Craig as he walked into the room. "The last thing we need is for these people to try and make a name for themselves by blowing something or someone up."

"I agree," said Jim. "We can count on you and your men to make this happen right?"

"You got it brother," said Craig.

Hans and Sam had been to all of the communities that were receiving help and protection. They had the trust and confidence of the leaders in all of them, or so they thought. The invincible men were honest and fair with everyone.

While visiting one of the protected communities, Sam was checking on the perimeter security and uninhabited buildings when he was confronted by a few men.

"Whatcha doing there buddy?" asked one of the men.

"Just making sure that everything is secure over here on the west side," Sam replied. "Was there anything I can help you guys with tonight?"

Sam had activated his radio and held down the transmitter, so Hans could hear the conversation. The mic was held open, so Hans could only listen and not respond.

The large German left what he was doing immediately, on his way to assist Sam. Hans had been able to get the gene therapy and Sam had not. If things were going sideways, he had to reach him in time to help.

"We were just wondering if you liked working for the people that have locked us up?" asked another man.

"I don't work for anyone," said Sam. "We all live and work together to reach the same goals buddy."

"And what would those goals be?" asked one of the men.

"Global peace and harmony, what else?" said Sam.

Hans walked around a building next to the barrier as the men were talking.

"There you are brother," said Hans. "What are you guys up too?"

"We were just getting to know each other," said Sam.

"Thanks for the info," said one of the men as they started walking away.

"What the hell was that about?" Hans asked Sam.

"I don't know man, but I think we need to add some security cameras inside the city walls and keep an eye on things."

"We can get a message to Craig when we get back to the ship," said Hans.

More people in most of the other communities were also acting strangely when the ships arrived periodically to check up on them or bring in supplies.

The group decided that along with new surveillance measures, they had to get someone inside one of the communities to find out what was going on. A community was selected, as was a person that would infiltrate it. The plan was set in motion, with no way to contact the person on the inside until they had collected information about the strange activity. Routine scans were done in each community and outlying areas for anything out of the ordinary. Heat signatures on thermal scans were getting the best results. When many bodies were seen in one area for an extended period, raids and searches were conducted there by suit soldiers. The searches turned up large weapons and ammo caches as well as explosives. People in those areas were questioned, but nobody would talk.

With no budgets to contend with or government oversight, the people left on the planet could do virtually whatever they wanted. The advanced humans had quelled much of the lawlessness and violence that lay in the wake of the worst devastation the current inhabitants of Earth had ever witnessed.

With the technology and other advancements they brought with them to help others, they were a godsend to most. Others saw them as the enemy, a people that wanted to rule over them just because they had the power. At no time did the people that had received the gene therapy treat anyone as a lesser species. They only brought help with them at every turn. They had to show the others that didn't agree that they brought with them all that was promised and more.

The agent that was selected to infiltrate the chosen community was in place, now it was a waiting game.

The Fides was on its way back from the comet mission. The core samples had not proven to be of any use even though the rock had come from a great distance away, possibly from the far reaches of the galaxy or beyond. The samples taken from Mars had proven to be the most resilient and impervious to anything they could throw at it so far.

With the right amount of tempering, the material could be made to be paper thin and still able to withstand anything they currently had.

Karen designed a lightweight suit that could be worn like an under layer of clothing. The pliability was amazing. Traditional encased projectile firearms were tested on it first in a laboratory setting hooked up to sensors. The material distributed the force of everything fired at it evenly, so that no trauma was inflicted on the user. Bladed objects were tested on it too and all broke with enough force. The repulsion technology would be incorporated with the new material so nothing would touch it, but if it did then the user would still be safe. After lab trials, human trials were next, and Steve volunteered for them.

The tests were to be conducted on the airstrip. The desert base was more suited for the trials, but Steve wanted to give the community a show. They had been working very hard to accomplish all of the goals set before them and a break was warranted.

Steve walked out to the range they had built after they got there and prepared to be fired upon. The demonstrator used a handgun, then an M4, a 240 Golf chambered in .308 full auto, and then the .50 cal. This one actually pushed Steve back, with its 690 grain bullets hitting him extremely hard with their repulsion force.

Next, a suit soldier fired an ion pulse weapon at him. The impact of one round threw him back a few feet when it connected with the repulsion of the suit. Steve got up after catching his breath, shaking his head, but still no penetrations. The show was spectacular, the test a success, and a massive barbeque followed. Another reason for a party was always welcome.

A small mining team was sent up to Mars aboard the Fortis to get more of the material that Ann had brought back, which she named Annimantium and added to the periodic table. With a sample of the material they could run it through a mass spectrometer then the sensors aboard the ship could detect pockets of it for mining. The material could be applied very thin and still retain its hardness and flexibility, so not as much would be needed for overlaying the suits and ships. A permanent mining colony was briefly discussed, but with so much happening on Earth, it was shelved for the time being.

More and more couples were emerging from within the community on the airstrip, as they all got to know one another. Ann warned the people that had the advanced intelligence that breeding with regular humans might turn out to be a bad choice. Not knowing how inter-breeding would work on a genetic level was risky. Ann and Simon decided that testing was the right thing to do, in order to know for sure. Two subjects from each sex were asked to participate with egg and sperm donations. Ann and Simon would inseminate the eggs in a lab and grow the fetus in order to better understand the viability. This would take time, but this was the safest way to find out compatibility.

The agent inside the chosen community was still out of reach after almost a month, and this was starting to concern some of the people eager to hear a report from the mission.

"How much longer should we wait?" Craig asked the others. "We haven't seen her on the cameras in almost a week. Something's wrong, I know it."

"Let's give it another forty-eight hours and then go into the city en force," said Doug.

"We might ruin any chance at finding out the plans of the resistance," said Chris.

"Nate says Samantha can handle herself, and I agree from what I've seen," said Jill. "Give her some more time."

Samantha was one of the best and brightest they had and could do things all of the others couldn't. She had somehow figured out how to hide her abilities. If she was hit, she bruised. If cut, she didn't heal right away. Being able to suppress her gift made her the perfect operative for any mission. Despite being able to do these things, she was very capable in other ways too.

The woman was the toughest some of the interrogators had ever seen, but everyone had their limits, and they knew this. The question was, would she submit before lying or dying?

"Do you think we're stupid little girl?" asked a very muscular man with the military buzz cut. He had been torturing Samantha for the last few days. "We know you work for those freaks; I can smell it on you."

"What do I have to do to prove to you that I am on your side?" slurred Samantha out of the corner of her fat lip. She opened up her right eye the best she could and looked up at the man, her left eye swollen shut. "I will do anything."

"I know you will Nadia, if that's your real name," said a tall thin man with short dark hair and glasses.

"It is," said Samantha. "I don't know why you are doing this to me. I just want to find my family."

"So," said the man. "Is this the reason you were asking so many questions in the bar?"

"Yes," said Samantha. "If joining your cause allows me to find my family, then I will help you."

"Will you kill for us? This man in particular," the man said as he showed her a picture of Steve.

"Who is he?" she asked.

"Just a thorn in our sides," said the tall man.

"Tell me what I need to do," Samantha told him.

"Release her and get her cleaned up," he told the muscular man.

Samantha was unbuckled from the torture chair she had been in and she fell to the floor. The large man picked up her broken, naked body and carried her out of the room and down a corridor to another room, where he left her with two women. He told them to care for her.

A strike team assembled for each of the three ships going to rescue Samantha. All would be crewed by soldiers in the suits made of the new lightweight, pliable material discovered on Mars. They headed for their separate coordinates around the city. The satellite just above that area of the country was feeding all the ships live feeds from above in conjunction with the cameras on the ground.

The forty-eight-hour window was almost up, when the orbiting satellite picked up Samantha's tracking device walking up into a structure from beneath it. As soon as she went underground, the signal was lost.

The ships were stopped just outside the city when they received the transmission from the small implanted tracker. She walked out of the building and into another one a few blocks down the road.

"Anything I can help you with?" asked the chubby, bald clerk sitting at the desk at the hotel lobby.

"I need a room," said Samantha.

"What do you have to trade?" asked the man, looking at her body and back to her bruised face.

She threw a Beretta 92 9mm handgun up on the counter and asked, "Will this work?"

"That will work just fine," said the clerk as he scooped the handgun off the counter discreetly, looking a little disappointed that she hadn't offered herself instead.

Guns were outlawed inside the communities, making them almost priceless. If anyone was caught with one, they were banished to outside of the walls. There was very little crime on the inside and most wanted it to stay that way.

Samantha took the key to her room from the man at the desk and slowly walked to the elevator. After she was in, she allowed herself to heal completely and was back to normal right away. When the elevator reached the sixth floor, she got out and quickly went to her room and immediately got into the shower to clean up.

The Intrepidus hovered above the tallest building in the city and lowered its ramp. Jake jumped a few feet to the rooftop and the ship flew off. He made his way to the lower level and onto the streets. He had unsuited and was back in street clothes. After reaching the hotel, he walked down the alley to the right of it and pulled open a locked door outside the service entrance, breaking the deadbolt with ease in the process. He made his way to the sixth floor by way of the emergency stairs and knocked on Samantha's door as she got out of the shower. She opened the door and was pleasantly surprised. Jake moved into the room, picked her up and carried her to the bed.

"Wait," she said. "Do you have coms with a ship?"

"I do," said Jake as he handed her the radio.

"Who is it?" she asked.

"It's Jim," he replied.

"Jim, it's Samantha."

"Go ahead," said Jim.

"I've been tasked with a kill order to prove my loyalty to the cause. The target is Steve."

"Why Steve?" he asked.

"I don't know," she said, "but they showed me his picture and I have one week to bring them proof of the assassination. I'll be getting on a ship to go look for my sister in two days as my cover."

"Roger that, and good work," said Jim.

Samantha turned off the radio, tossed it on the chair by the bathroom and looked at Jake. "Now, where were we?" she asked, taking off her robe and exposing her naked body.

"A kill order for me?" asked Steve, the next morning at the base in the desert. "I really don't understand why."

"We don't either," said Jim. "We will of course have to make it look real and have some witnesses."

Knowing that they had little time to put a plan together, they started immediately. Samantha couldn't just shoot Steve, who would recover, she would have to cut his head off and this is where Simon and others would come in. She would have to bring proof of the kill to the leaders of the resistance. A video recording would have to do, because she couldn't bring his body back. If they had the right technology, they could figure out a fake so it had to be an original and look real.

The stage was set back at the base. Samantha was to ask to speak with Steve and would be allowed to. He would be working in a lab and there would be sharp objects that she would have access to while there. She would tell him that she was doing a documentary on the new people and their powers giving her an excuse to film their interaction. She would grab a knife on the table when Steve wasn't looking and stab him multiple times. Steve would fall to the floor and she would get behind him to cut his head off as she was instructed to do by the resistance. Her camera would fall off the table during the struggle and that's when the body double would be placed where Steve had been. She would set the camera back up and cut off his head. She would then cut off his right index finger to bring back DNA proof, which was really Steve's finger and more than they had asked for.

All the witnesses were in on the scenario, so when it came time to execute the plan, it worked like clockwork. Samantha was soon on her way back toward the resistance base. She had hopefully proven herself loyal to the cause and would be hailed as a hero. She of course modestly told everyone that she was just doing what she could to help out.

Chapter Eleven: Us or Them

Some didn't understand the reasons for a resistance. The people were protected and now had many of the same comforts that had been taken away from them years before. Others understood why the people were acting the way they were.

Throughout human history, civilizations would rise up over the ages and when they became powerful, they wanted to rule over everyone. After the bombs fell, many saw the possibility for a new start for mankind. Then the advanced humans entered the arena and stopped all of the militias and military factions from rising to power This is when resistance started. It began in an infant form at first and grew from there. This was perceived to be a threat to the invincibles and the plans they had. No matter how it happened, the resistance had to be stopped.

"Our new recruit did a wonderful job completing her mission, general," said Seth Jackson to the commander of the resistance. Seth, a former Special Forces operator, known for his brutality toward the enemy, had planned the mission to assassinate Steve. Seth was a man in his mid forties, just under six feet tall, with short dark hair and a scruffy unshaven face. His look was one of terror to most that came in contact with him.

"She did do a wonderful job," said the general, agreeing with Seth. The general was the only name that people knew the short, stocky man by. He was their leader and did a wonderful job at fighting back at the people that had enslaved them.

"What's our next move?" asked Seth.

"I'm working on that right now," said the general. "We're getting DNA conformation from our friends in that undisclosed location we recently spoke of. I can't plan our next move without it."

"Roger that sir. I'm going to the bar for the night. Let me know if you need me."

Seth was the manager of the community tavern at night. The corn and wheat fields were providing not only food, but a nice source for moonshine. Others had built stills behind the building now used for the bar. The people of the community needed a release after working all day and this was the place to be. Seth named the place the End of the World Bar and Grill. Most thought the name fitting.

"What will you have tonight sweetheart?" Seth asked Samantha, who he knew as Nadia, as she walked up to the bar and took a seat.

"What are my choices?" she asked him.

"Corn or wheat flavor darling," he replied with a grin.

"Corn," said Samantha with a smile.

She took a shot of the moonshine and immediately spit it back out all over Seth. The others in the bar laughed loudly.

"I am so sorry," said Samantha to Seth, who was wiping his shirt off with a towel from the bar.

"It happens all the time," he said back. "Try it again, and swallow quickly this time don't breathe right away. In fact, exhale after swallowing. After the first couple of shots you'll be used to it and all your taste buds will have gone numb."

Samantha did as she was instructed by Seth and confirmed that it worked. More people arrived as the night progressed and Samantha acted like she was very drunk after about four hours. Jake wandered into the bar after some time and asked the other bartender about Nadia. He pointed Jake in her direction just as Seth was trying to leave with her.

"Just a minute buddy," Jake said to Seth as he walked up to them.

Seth turned around and saw Jake standing there. He sat Samantha down in a chair, which she fell right back out of laughing.

"Something I can help you with friend?" inquired Seth.

"That's my sister-in-law," said Jake, "and I don't think she's in any condition to leave with you, friend."

"Can you prove your claim?" asked Seth.

"She has a tattoo of a dolphin on her right hip," said Jake.

Seth pulled her shirt up and skirt down a little to look. Sure enough, there was a dolphin.

"Just how do you know about the tattoo if you're her brother-in-law?" asked Seth.

"Her sister, my wife, had the same tattoo buddy. They got them together one night and I was there. Now, back off and let us pass," said Jake.

Seth reluctantly let Jake take Samantha and they left out the front door with everyone watching them. Jake carried her two blocks and put her down.

"Damn you're heavy girl," he said to her.

Samantha smacked him on his arm. "Funny," she said.

"Are you okay?" Jake asked her.

"I am now," she said as she pushed him against the building they were standing in front of and kissed him, rough.

"Let's take this inside," said Jake. "We don't want to blow your cover; I am your brother-in-law you know."

They went into the hotel separately and met up in Samantha's room.

On the desert base, Steve was sitting around with Doug and Chris. Steve had been isolated in a private room after the attack, which everyone thought had really claimed his life. Unfortunately, even Karen thought he was dead. They needed to flush out the moles on the airstrip and base. The resistance knew too much for just being a ragtag group of prior military guys. They had to have people on the inside and technology helping them on the outside.

"How long do you anticipate it will be before I can leave here and go see Karen," Steve asked Doug.

"We have to figure out who they flipped or who they used to infiltrate our group," said Doug.

"I understand," said Steve, "but Karen not knowing the truth..."

"Will make the whole scenario more believable," said Chris. "Take it easy and let us figure this out. We still need to know why they targeted you over anyone else."

"Because I'm so smart and good looking," Steve joked. "I want to know just as much, if not more than you guys."

The next morning, Samantha got a knock at her door. Jake quickly got dressed and threw some of the bed's blankets on the couch to make it look like he had slept there. Samantha had just gotten out of the shower and went to the door in a robe.

"Good morning Seth," she said after opening the door. "What can I do for you?"

Seth looked around the room and saw Jake on the couch. He nodded to Jake and looked back at Samantha.

"A mutual friend would like to talk to you Nadia," he said to her.

"Let me get dressed and I'll be right with you."

She invited him in, but he just stood by the door waiting. Jake got up and walked over to the windows, looking out over the city.

"So how long have you been here Seth?" asked Jake.

"Long enough to know my place buddy," replied Seth. "You staying long?"

"I'm staying as long as I need to. So, where does Nadia need to go?"

"Someone we know just wants to talk to her, no big deal. I'll have her back in no time."

Samantha walked out of the bathroom and told Seth she was ready. "I'll be back soon Jake," she said.

With the new ID cards and surveillance cameras in place, not much happened on the old airstrip that wasn't known about. Narrowing down the leak in each area wouldn't be too difficult. Many people had already been taken off the possible candidate list. Most of the prior military and some of the civilians that recently became new members of a community were suspect.

As more people in each community were dropped from suspicion, the field narrowed down. Those people were watched more carefully, with the idea that the guilty parties would inevitably slip up sooner or later. On the airstrip, it was down to one man and one woman.

Carol had been with the community for more than a year and had gone out on many working parties and humanitarian missions. She had access to most things on the compound and had left the area many times. She was a nice person and seemed to want to help out with everything. She had lost everyone she ever knew when the bombs fell, which had taken a toll on her. She was in her early forties, but appeared to be in her sixties. Her hair was a mixture of gray and brown. The bags under her eyes made her look like she never slept. She had been a heavy drinker in her younger years and it showed.

Michael, a young guy in his twenties with short hair and a baby face was newer and had been there for a few months. He had a military background and a few times had been found in different areas than those he was supposed to be working in. He would say that he was lost because he was new, but this was only believable for so long.

After days of surveillance, it turned out Carol was the leak on the airstrip. Another woman had been caught on the desert base too. The resistance had figured that a woman would be trusted more easily, and could therefore infiltrate most places more easily. The women were brought together in a room on the base and allowed to interact. It turned out that they didn't know each other. Both were tested for compatibility to the gene therapy and tests came back positive. The reward was worth the risk.

A few days after the two women were confined to the room and questioned. Ann walked in and offered them the inoculation. They thought it was a trick, but finally relented.

"Why would you just give us enhanced abilities and advanced intelligence?" asked Carol.

Alexandra, Alex for short, wondered the same thing. She was in her early twenties and had short blonde hair on top of an athletic build. She was very attractive and was able to get into many places that she wasn't supposed to have access to by using what she had.

"We have been blessed with the greatest gift anyone could have been bestowed on us," said Ann. "They have shown us the way and we have shared all of this with you and the others."

"I don't understand," said Carol.

Doug brought the lamp-looking device that Steve had built into the room and the holographic image emerged; the recording played for the women. The hope was that they would see the potential and want to be a part of the future.

The two resistance operatives couldn't believe what they had seen and heard.

"This can't be real," said Alex. "All of this advanced technology came from another planet? How far away do these people live?"

"We don't have all of the answers," said Ann. "We believe because it is true and you will understand once you have what we have."

Carol was ready to be inoculated, but Alex was still skeptical. She hadn't been with the group as long, or seen as much. Alex had lost everyone she had ever known or loved, which was another reason the resistance had chosen her. They told her who the enemy was and she believed them. She was vulnerable and easily manipulated, so she thought these were just more enemy tactics to fool her.

Doug, Ann and a few others discussed the pros and cons of just giving Alex the therapy without her compliance. They figured that it had to be done or they would just have more people working against them down the road.

Carol was inoculated and so was Alex, against her will. After the twenty-four hour quarantine time, they were both escorted to the command center of the base and everything was revealed to them. Alex now fully understood the good that they could do, how they could rebuild the planet to its former glory, and much more.

With the help of Alex and Carol, more people from the resistance were brought into the light. Ann picked the people that would get the gene therapy. There were some people that she knew right away would not fit in with the rest. The resistance movement slowly became a thing of the past. Rebuilding humanity would be easier now without resistance from those still wanting to destroy it. Power in the wrong hands was the problem before, and the cause of so much war and death all throughout history.

Some people wanted all the answers to their questions before being given the gene therapy. She got a large group of enhanced people and candidates together for a discussion.

"I knew one day I would have someone ask the right questions, and it has happened," said Ann. "There are some of you that want to know what's in this magical serum we have created. Well, it's not magical, it's all natural. We combined the elements from many plants and animals on Earth with the right properties. Starfish can regenerate; birds and other animals can see very well, others have better hearing than others. We took the best of everything and combined it all on a cellular level so that our bodies wouldn't reject it. Some humans have proven resilient to this, and we have proven it can be very dangerous for everyone if they are injected. Once inoculated, you will be able to understand all of this to its full extent."

There were still a few questions, but most people understood enough to want to become better.

Chapter Twelve: New Beginnings

Once some of the newest people had been given the gene therapy and were brought into the fold, everything fell into place. The holographic recording from the machine that Steve had built was shown to more and more people and it all became clear to the newcomers. The only way to bring the human population back from the darkness and into the light was to reach the goals set by the ones that had come before them. With the new knowledge, they realized they could achieve great things. They were already on their way, but now had the right path presented to them.

The human population on Earth was now small compared to the billions of people that populated it before, but the planet would soon bounce back in every way. The advanced technology and intelligence would move everything along faster, and no one would be left out in the cold suffering ever again.

"I can't believe you had to fake your death," said Karen, who was very happy to have Steve back home.

"Everything is back on track now," said Steve. "The resistance led by the old government of the United States is now willing to move forward for all mankind. Other governments in other parts of the world are being shown the way also. The people that couldn't see the big picture took an early retirement to live out their days."

"What do you mean?" asked Karen.

Steve sat down and explained it all to Karen.

An island in the Pacific Ocean was picked for those that still didn't want to work with the rest. An ion pulse generator was installed for their use and they had access to all the supplies they would need to build their own society. The island was stocked with wildlife for them to use as they saw fit. This was a group decision, made by those who had received the gene therapy, and they all felt it was the best thing that could be done for all mankind. Banishing people because they wouldn't comply was not something that they had planned, but had to happen for the sake of humankind. There would always be some sort of resistance to certain ideas or groups; this was unfortunately inevitable, but also avoidable.

According to the intelligence reports that the resistance had received before, when the movement was gaining momentum, Steve was a leader of the people that they were against. That's why they wanted to kill him. They had plans for Jim, Doug and others if they had been allowed to go that far. They knew that cutting their heads off was the only way that they and the other powerful ones could be killed. The brutality that those people had showed was considered a lack of intelligence, and they went to the island too.

Samantha was back among the group on the base, with her ship and crew members aboard the Fortis. The job that she had done for the good of everyone would not be forgotten. She had proven her worth to all of them and brought Jake even closer to her.

The fifth cruiser-class ship meant for Doug's command was near completion. Work on it had slowed dramatically during the investigations, when the potential for attack was high. Security had been tight and not many people were allowed to work in the sensitive areas like life support, navigation and weapons. Jim was asked many times what he would call the new ship, but he always said he was still considering what to call it.

"Are you still thinking about a name for your ship?" Chris asked Doug one day as they were working on it.

"I think I finally have a good name," said Doug.

"What did you come up with?"

"The Fidelis will be her name. It's a word from the Marine Corps motto, Semper Fidelis, or always faithful."

"I think faithful is fitting," said Chris. "Any word yet on who is going to command the sixth ship? It is the last one."

"We were going to see if you wanted the job," said Jim, who walked onto the bridge of the Fidelis.

"You want me to command one of the ships that will make up the big one? The one that's going to leave Earth?" asked Chris.

"Well, if you're the commander then you'll have to come with us," said Jim with a smile.

"I'm going to have to talk this over with Kerri. Rachael and Silvia are almost adults and...wow," said Chris, still slightly in shock at the offer. "I'll give you my answer soon."

"That's all we can ask," said Doug.

The super computer built in conjunction with the satellites orbiting the planet and monitoring everything was moved from the airstrip to the desert base. The command and control center already in place there was easily converted to display everything happening around the globe. It was just like the other, but better. They could focus on other projects now that a resistance wasn't knocking at the proverbial door. Vital plans were set in motion and couldn't continue without everyone on board. It would take time to reach the goals, years in fact, but would be worth all the effort.

There was still no other contact in the solar system, not since the probe had left. The satellite early warning system that Steve had designed was now in orbit in Saturn's outer ring and was working well. It had picked up many interesting rocks and radiation waves entering the system since it was placed there.

The airstrip had been home to many people for years, but it was time to find a more permanent place to construct the ships. A proper plant was planned for the sole purpose of producing ships that the entire planet's population could utilize eventually. A research and development area was set up at the Mojave base, headed by Steve and Karen. Everything would take time, but for the most part, time was no longer an issue.

Ann and Doug's son Potremo was walking, writing and solving equations that they put on paper or a tablet for him. He was still going to see Gary and Trevor on a regular basis for checkups. He was the world's youngest child prodigy in any area. The boy was the child of parents who had both altered their genome, a product of what the other race across the vast expanse of outer space had failed to achieve, until it was too late for their kind.

A regular school had been set up for all of the new kids that had come with their parents to work at the airstrip. With more qualified people in the community, the kids had a better opportunity to learn and achieve. The move to the base would be a big one for most people and a building was set aside for a new school house.

Karen was glad to have Steve back home with her and De Novo full time. They had been making up for lost time in every way, especially in the bedroom. Karen was feeling strange one morning and went to see Gary. After a few tests, Gary stopped talking about the weather. He'd been filling Karen in on the new place he and Nancy would be going for awhile.

"Karen, you're pregnant," said Gary. "Congratulations."

"I am?" said Karen, a little surprised.

"Karen, you're a grown woman and a mother already, but if I need to remind you about how this happens..." he joked.

"You know that's not why I'm surprised," she said seriously. "We were hoping that this wouldn't happen for awhile longer. With all that's been going on, another baby?"

"I suppose you should let Steve in on the good news," said Gary.

Karen would be having the second child of a superior race of humans. The people that had altered their genome were essentially hybrids, but these new children they were having would be pure.

"That's wonderful!" said Steve excitedly when Karen gave him the news about the pregnancy.

"I'm happy too," said Karen, "but I was hoping to be able to help more in the new R&D wing that we're supposed to be running."

"You're going to be able to help out as much as you want until the baby comes."

"And after?" asked Karen.

"I heard that Theresa and Bill are expecting a baby too and will be moving to the base soon. We'll need a nursery and daycare, maybe she would want to head it up. It wouldn't hurt to ask her," said Steve.

"I'll talk to her soon. I want to rekindle our friendship. Ever since we were all inoculated, many of our friends have given us the cold shoulder. Now we'll have something in common again, just maybe," said Karen.

The transition from one place to the next for most had become second nature, but it was still something that no one really wanted to do.

"We go where the work is," Bill said to Theresa while he was packing his clothes.

"I know, but the kids and I have grown to love this place."

"The base will just be temporary until we get the manufacturing plant up and running. There's talk of building high rise apartments close to the plants. This place will be a ghost town before long. Besides you have to follow your husband right?"

"Bill, are you proposing to me?" asked Theresa surprised.

"I am, if you'll have me," he said. "I wouldn't feel right if I didn't make an honest woman out of you."

Theresa said yes and gave Bill a big hug and kiss.

"A wedding, will we be having one?" she asked suddenly. "What will I wear if we do?"

"I'll talk to everyone and set it all in motion," said Bill. "I know we'll be busy, but I'll make sure you have the best wedding ever."

Theresa was glowing as she said goodbye to Bill.

Once more people found out about the wedding, there was quite a bit of excitement in the air. They were all getting ready to move, but there was more and more talk about Bill and Theresa's wedding.

Nancy offered to make the wedding dress and others offered to help with many other parts of the upcoming event. The mood was joyous, but tired at the same time. Most of the people in the now large community had been working nonstop to reach the construction goals, and looked forward to taking a much needed break. The base had set aside three days for R&R and the wedding.

Bill and Theresa hadn't been compatible with the gene therapy, so they'd felt like they didn't belong for the longest time. A surprise honeymoon awaited them after the ceremony. No one that knew would tell them anything about it.

Work continued as more people were shuttled to the base and other communities close by. Some people didn't want to live on a military base and were welcomed in the closest communities A few short weeks later when everyone had gotten settled, preparations were made for the ceremony. The planning and set up took a few days. People helped on their off time to get it all done in time.

A small detail manned the command center while the festivities were going on. Most of them wanted to attend, but security was still paramount. The people inside the command center watched the whole thing on a large monitor. The ceremony and reception were held in the same building and after a few hours of dancing and merriment, it was time to leave.

After the reception, the Fides flew into the area just outside the dance floor, which had been constructed outside the building where the wedding was held. The ramp was lowered and the newlyweds were asked to walk onboard. Ann was going to fly them to the moon for a few days and then wherever on the planet they wanted to go for another few days. Bets were on for a trip to a tropical island somewhere. They wouldn't know where they were headed until they boarded her ship.

Ann and Doug would be taking them on their own. Since they were just going a small distance and wouldn't need all the other crew members to run the ship, they figured they could handle it. The ship rose above the base and slowly gained altitude. Bill and Theresa walked onto the bridge and saw the viewing window was open for them.

"This is incredible," said Theresa. "I've flown in these ships many times, but have never looked out the viewing window."

"Thank you so much for this," said Bill. "So, where do you plan on taking us?"

"How does the moon sound for a honey-moon?" Ann asked them smiling. "You will be all alone on the ship, except for us of course. Steve and Karen made you two suits so you can venture out onto the lunar surface if you want, but just relax otherwise. We've made a room up for you in the cabin. We took all of the seats out and made it into a honeymoon suite. The viewing window controls will be yours to operate."

"Please take a seat as we exit the atmosphere and become weightless," said Doug. "The trip will just take a few hours. Once we reach our cruising speed, you're more than welcome to float around."

Bill and Theresa had not been in space yet and immediately got out of their seats to experience weightlessness once they were told they could.

"I never thought I would be able to do this," said Bill, "it's like a dream."

"It's one of the most amazing things I've ever experienced," said Doug. "It never gets old."

Theresa was laughing as she floated around the cabin. Her wedding dress looked huge as she twirled around the bridge.

"We should have brought a camera," she commented.

"I've been recording everything on the ship since you two boarded," said Ann. "You'll get the video card and be able to edit it and pull stills off of it too."

"You're not going to be recording in our room are you?" Theresa asked seriously.

"No, the cameras have been covered in that part of the ship," said Doug smiling. "You two can do whatever you want and no one will know."

The Fides flew on for the next few hours and finally got to the spot that Ann wanted to take them on the lunar surface.

"Please sit down and buckle up as we enter the gravitational pull of the moon and land," Ann said.

After landing, Bill and Theresa had to get used to the smaller amount of gravity on the surface. They got settled in the room that had been turned into a honeymoon suite and enjoyed all that was left for them.

The next morning, Ann woke the couple over the intercom.

"Hey you two, I have a nice brunch made for you in the kitchen. Will you be joining us or do you want breakfast in bed?"

"We'll be there in a few minutes," said Bill as he looked over at Theresa and smiled.

They got up and went to meet Ann and Doug in the dining area. They couldn't believe the food that was laid out for them. Pastries and fruits as well as bacon and sausage covered the table. After a fantastic meal, they thanked their hosts and retired back to their room.

Their second night on the moon, Ann decided to go into orbit for a few hours, to let them float about the ship while and enjoy some more weightlessness. They would be able to enjoy the view of the Earth and the moon. Theresa was excited about being able to experience so much.

The ship took off slowly and established a low orbit where everything was in view. They would have four hours and Bill had every intention of taking advantage of all of it.

"Have you ever heard of the mile high club?" he asked his new bride.

"I have," said Theresa. "Isn't that where people have sex on a plane in the small and stinky lavatory?"

"It is when you're on a plane, but what about a spaceship orbiting the moon? We could be the first couple to join the million mile high club," said Bill with a smile.

"I don't know, what if Ann or Doug come in here?"

"They're probably doing the same thing right now," said Bill. "They won't be disturbing us."

Theresa relented, so Bill dimmed the lights and turned on some music to make the mood more romantic. They slowly undressed each other and floated around the cabin having what they would later tell certain people, was "the best sex ever," until they hit a wall. They were both laughing about the incident and floated back into each other's arms. Their clothing was floating all over the cabin beside them the whole time.

A few hours later, Ann announced that they would be landing. The next day they would be able to leave the ship and explore the surface.

Chapter Thirteen: Preparations

A light guard of a half dozen suit soldiers were left watching the airstrip and all the machinery while the remaining occupants were shuttled to the base. Eventually they'd be taken to the future sites of the plants for constructing more ships and other vital components that would help rebuild their civilization. They were all relocated to the base first and from there, they went to work. There were four stages. First came the construction of a wall around the chosen area for security, and second the buildings to house the ion pulse generators. The third phase was the smelting plants and the fourth the fabrication facilities. The plants would be running twenty-four hours a day and there would be three over lapping eight-hour crews. The workers would live on the base in the Mojave Desert and be shuttled to work continually. Some people had chosen to live in surrounding communities instead of the base. They would be picked up before their shifts started and go to the facility.

With the new addition of people that had gotten the gene therapy, there were now more men and women that could take on important roles in preparing all aspects of the base, construction and ship crews. Now that more people had access to the ships and key areas of the base a measure was implemented to make sure that only qualified personnel were able to access certain areas, or use the advanced technology. Karen was the one that brought this need to the main group's attention.

"If we make all the ship's functions and those in vital areas of the facilities readable only by us in the ancient Latin language, I believe that we would restrict access to only those qualified, and in turn make everything run much smoother and safer," said Karen in a meeting of the original leaders, the ones who got inoculated first.

"This would also make things easier from a security standpoint," said Craig.

"I thought we wanted all the people of Earth to be able to eventually have everything that has been given to us?" questioned Kerri.

"Yes and no," said Ann. "We will still make all of their lives better in every way, but the destructive nature of humans has to stop, and I like Karen's idea to help curb this."

"Ann's right," said Jim. "If you give certain people the power that can destroy or rule people, they will take it, and eventually this civilization will be back in the same place, wondering how it all happened. It is, after all, human nature, and proven all throughout our history."

"This is why we started the colony on the island in the Pacific Ocean," said Chris.

A few people nodded their heads in agreement after Chris spoke up.

"We will implement Karen's idea on a wide scale just as soon as it can be done. With the ships being so intricate already, they would be the last things that a normal person could figure out. Facilities will be tackled first and the ships last," said Doug.

All in attendance agreed to the new protocols and would follow Karen's lead. She agreed to draw up the plan that would produce the best results.

Security and trust was essential in order to make everything work. Once the new plants were up and running, the sixth and final ship could be built. With so many more people it was a good plan.

Chris had made his decision about taking command of the last cruiser, and Kerri was fully behind him. He had spent much of his adult life in the pursuit of going into space and exploration of the same. This would be the ultimate endeavor for him and she was all for it. Their girls needed to make up their mind whether they would go with them. They both had a place on Earth and on the ship. Either way, life as they used to know it would never be theirs again.

Aside from some essential personnel on the base to monitor the three dimensional viewing screens in the command and control center, and a skeleton crew for the ship that would stay behind, everyone went to help with the construction of the new facilities. Suit soldiers were dropped into areas around the perimeter for security until a wall could be built. All the available ships would take crews out to bring in material for construction while other crews were on the ground working on the walls.

Once the walls were close to completion, the buildings that would house the ion pulse generators could be started. They would be constructed half a mile away from where the future sight of the smelting plants and fabrication facilities would be. An underground power grid was to be put in place that could power everything on the site.

After the shell of the smelting plants and fabrication buildings were built, then the equipment from the airstrip could be brought in and installed, along with the new equipment currently being built.

The work was steady, and with the hundreds of people that were working on all the projects, it all got done pretty fast and safe. With all that was going on, there had been no accidents on any of the construction sites. That could change at any moment, but so with many of the people in possession of advanced intelligence and healing ability, the likelihood was small.

"Well, I just got word that the walls are up and the generators are online," Jim said to James, who was sitting next to him on the flight deck of the Intrepidus.

"Fantastic," said James, "it only took three weeks. We can really get more done now. The wall was the largest project that we have I believe."

The Intrepidus was on its last run for the night with Ann in the Fides and another load flying right beside them.

Scrap material was getting more difficult to find, metal that wasn't radioactive that is. They would have to start mining raw material soon, which would take more time to set up. For now, longer trips to other continents would have to work. Once all the plants were set up, they could focus on the raw materials they needed. The technology that the Fortis had aboard would aid the mining crews in locating large ore deposits for recovery. The mass spectrometer that they had installed and modified for locating the Annimantium on Mars was a fantastic tool. Once a sample of the desired material needed was analyzed, the machine would locate it as the ship flew above the ground. Each ship would eventually have this instrument at their disposal. The ships would be able to get mining crews into even the most remote areas. Time consuming roads would not have to be built. The areas mined would be smaller due to the precision of finding deposits.

With the perimeter walls completed, more people could help with the construction of the buildings for the different plants. Within a few more weeks, most of the projects were done and equipment was brought in to be hooked up and brought online.

Construction on the sixth and final ship was about to start, and many were looking forward to getting back to fabricating and smelting. This is what they had been doing on the airstrip from the time they first arrived there, and they wanted to try out the new facility. Chris was ready to oversee the construction and add his final touches to it when they got there. He had already come up with a name and announced it at dinner the night before they started on it.

"I have a small announcement," said Chris as he stood up in the dining area at the base. "I know most of you won't be as excited about this as you were about the wedding we just had, but I've decided to call the cruiser I will command the Paratus, which means ready."

"Good choice," said Doug, "very fitting."

Most of the people in the dining area cheered.

Work was going well and the people in the new facilities had much more room to work in. Workers from every shift were in better spirits after taking the much needed time off. Better equipment and more people to help with the work kept them happy too. With three shifts overlapping and less time on the clock than they were used to, the shifts went by much faster. Everyone looked forward to more time to spend with loved ones, and time off to relax, while still getting the same amount of work done.

There was a stationary satellite in a low geosynchronous orbit above the newly built construction facility. It was placed there to monitor everything in a twenty-five mile radius around the walls. This was a vital area and had to be protected. The satellite cluster monitoring the planet already did a good job, but this area was a priority. The base in the Mojave had one too.

An alarm sounded one afternoon as outside sensors were tripped and the suit soldiers on duty climbed the stairs as fast as they could to reach the landing pad on top of the fabrication center. That extension of the building was made just for security and medevac purposes. If someone got hurt, they could be flown to the base quickly. The four soldiers reached the pad and synchronized their HUDs with the satellite. There was a vehicle with a lone man in it, as far as they could tell, heading toward the outside the wall. Even though he couldn't get in, they wanted to investigate the reason he was there. This would be the most excitement any of them had had in months.

The four soldiers leaped from the tower and their suits' jet packs and stabilizing thrusters kicked in. They leveled out and out came small wings from different areas of their suits for further stabilization. Two soldiers went off to the right flank and two went to the left. They flew high above the facility and walls of the compound.

"This is sierra one to bravo squad, I have the tango in sight," said Joe as he flew toward the truck.

"Why can't you just say hey guys, I see the dude and the truck, let's go check it out?" asked Tom, one of the newest people to get inoculated. He was young and had no military background. He continually joked with those that did.

"Sierra four if you can't follow protocol then you shouldn't be here," said Joe.

"I'm just messing with ya boss, I've been practicing that ponotec alphabet thing."

"It's called the phonetic alphabet, and you'd better get it soon or I'll send you back to the base to guard the perimeter and the desert," said Joe

"Roger that," said Tom.

The four men flew down and landed, surrounding the truck.

"This is a restricted area," said Joe in a commanding voice as he walked toward the man. "You'll have to turn around and leave immediately."

"Those are some pretty cool suits," said the man as he took off his black cowboy hat. He had long dark hair pulled back in a ponytail, and looked to be in his fifties. He sat on the tailgate and lit up a cigar.

"Sir, you will have to leave the area now," said Joe again sternly.

"I've been watching this whole show, and I've been wondering if you needed any more help. So... take me to your leader," said the man smiling. "I've always wanted to say that."

"I will not ask you again," said Joe approaching the truck with Tom beside him.

The man turned around, brought up an old M79 40 mm grenade launcher, and fired it before anyone could react. Joe and Tom were thrown back after the airburst explosion sent out what they would later learn was an electromagnetic wave. The other two soldiers quickly brought their ion pulse cannons up and pointed them at the man by the truck.

"Easy boys," he said. "This baby is only a one shot deal. I just had to try it out. My names Holliday, Major

Holliday to be exact and I'm really wanting you to take me to the man in charge."

Joe and Tom slowly got back up off the ground and regained their senses. They walked over to hear the last of what the major said.

"Control, this is sierra one, I need a ship to retrieve us on the south-west side of the wall by the old highway," said Joe internally on the coms, which were static at this point.

"Roger that sierra one," said a woman's voice. "Flight time to your position is ten minutes."

The Fortis arrived shortly after Joe made the call for retrieval. A small contingent came out to take the major into custody and they all got on board. The ramp to the cargo bay was left down as the ship took the security detail back to the tower. The four soldiers exited the ship once the ramp was just above the landing pad and then it left.

"What the hell just happened back there?" asked Tom as his visor on his helmet opened up.

"I'm not sure, but we'll find out, I guarantee it," said Joe as they walked back to the security room.

The whole encounter with Major Holliday was captured on video by the stationary satellite and the helmet cameras of the suit soldiers. The Fortis flew in and picked the man up to take him back to the base. The videos would be reviewed while he was in a detention room. He would be questioned later as to what kind of weapon had disabled the soldiers. The threat was deemed the highest priority.

Chapter Fourteen: Disruptions

"Do you have any idea why we're getting so much interference from the satellites on the light side and not the dark side?" Ben asked Doug.

"What kind of readings are you getting from the satellites facing the sun?"

"Everything is fuzzy. Poor picture and video quality," said Ben.

"No, I mean like x-rays, gamma-rays, radiation. We need to know about solar activity to figure out what's going on," said Doug. "Those are more than likely the problem on the light side of the Earth. There have been some reports of problems with communications in certain areas. The atmosphere will protect us down here from most of the radiation, but if there is a massive flare, we'll all be in trouble."

"It does make sense that the trouble would just be on the sunny side," said Ben. "We should have interruptions planet-wide if it's solar flares, but more on that side."

We'll figure out what's causing this and fix it, said Doug.

They decided to take a few ships up and perform some upgrades to the satellites. They needed to be protected from solar flares. The ion pulse cannons they had on board and repulsion technology in the shielding would already protect the satellites from most other threats. The material found on Mars should do the job of shielding them better.

While the preparations were made to better protect the satellites, many more places around the planet were reporting interference with electronics. There was defiantly more solar activity going on than they originally thought. Chris mentioned that the ozone layer in certain spots was thinner, letting in more radiation in those areas. Everything was taken into consideration.

The Intrepidus was sent on a separate mission to gather information on the strange solar activity while the others reinforced the satellites and other vital pieces of technology. Jim picked a skeleton crew out from all the people assigned to his ship. They left just as soon as they could get scrap material unloaded and prepare to go. They would all wear their suits for more protection if they needed it. The small crew was soon on their way, hopefully to make a difference.

On their way through the exosphere, they encountered quite a bit of unexpected turbulence.

"This shouldn't be happening," said Jim to the crew. "Everyone hang on tight."

Without any warning, all the systems in the ship and suits went offline. The ship was still moving, but no longer accelerating. About twenty seconds later, everything started working again. They would learn later that many systems on the planet had fluctuated at about the same time.

"What the hell was that?" asked Craig.

"I think that was a massive solar flare," said Jim, "but it shouldn't have affected our systems like that. We have the new shielding on the hull and it shouldn't have penetrated it."

"Let's get closer to the sun and take some readings," said James. "Certain electromagnetic currents are getting through and we need to find out how."

"On our way," said Jim as he brought the ship about on a course toward the sun.

Once the ship was a few hours from Earth, Jim stopped the engines and started scanning with all instruments. Steve and James had gone up to assist with the mission. Their understanding of radiation and the equipment would come in handy.

"I'm picking up two very large sun spots around the equator," said James.

"From what I've read in the data base, our sun should be in the minimum part of its solar cycle at this time," said Steve.

"Well, these active regions are sending out flares that are in excess of 100 million degrees Kelvin and I see no end in sight for now," replied James.

"There's nothing we can do but hope the cycle slows down soon and doesn't escalate," said Jim. "Get all the readings you can and let's get back. I don't like being this close."

Steve and James got all they could and Jim turned the ship around to head back to Earth.

The solar activity continued for days and slowly diminished. Everything was recorded into the database for further study.

The ships sent to retrofit the satellites got the job done quickly. Most of the suit soldiers were getting very good at spacewalking. With the jetpacks and stabilizing thrusters that Steve and his team had designed, it made maneuvering in space very easy.

The work in the new fabrication facility on the last ship had continued as much as it could while they were gone. The pace was brought back to normal once the ships were able to ferry in more supplies.

The man that had disabled Joe and Tom with an unknown weapon outside the walls of the production facility was left in a cell for weeks in hopes that he would be more willing to talk once they let him out. Bread and water were the only things he was allowed to have. Periods of darkness and very bright hot lights were introduced and he still didn't offer any information. Torture was not an option, but to deprive someone the basics would eventually drive them to releasing information to get it back. This technique had worked already with others and was used often. Torture didn't work for many reasons, so alternatives were used instead.

The satellite pictures showed the direction from which the man had driven his truck, but a search of the area turned up nothing. The whole vehicle and everything inside was inspected, but nothing was found to aid them in understanding what kind of weapon he'd fired at the soldiers from his launcher.

The major was brought out of his cell and taken to a visitation room one day. He was left there alone for a few hours before Doug entered.

"Finally, are you the man in charge?" asked the major. "Do you think I could get some bread and water? I'm hungry and very parched."

"I can answer your questions," said Doug, "and you can eat later."

"Okay, and you are?"

"Doug Stockton, and who are you, really?" asked Doug.

"I am who I say I am son. You're an astronaut right, commander? I thought you were older."

"I need to know who you are and what kind of weapon you used on our soldiers. Those suits were designed to withstand anything and you disabled them easily. Now tell me how," said Doug.

"It was pretty cool wasn't it? I've heard the stories about how bullets just bounce right off those suits and I figured the technology had to have some kind of electric current around it. I didn't have to be a rocket scientist to figure that one out."

"But you are a scientist," said Ann as she walked into the room. "You're Dr. Albert Holliday, United States Army. You held the rank of major while on active duty and had many technological breakthroughs for the government. You left early in your career, citing irreconcilable differences with your peers. Isn't that the word used in divorces?

"Hot stuff did her homework," said the major as he pointed at Ann, "and yes it was a marriage that had reached its end. They wouldn't let me run my department the way it needed to be run, and I never got credit for my work in the private sector."

"Watch yourself," warned Doug.

"Is she your woman? Let me know when you're done with her, I can think of a few ways she could be entertaining," he replied while smiling at Ann.

Doug left the room at Ann's request and the major smiled at him as he walked out the door.

"Just us sweet cheeks," said Holliday.

"Are you always this rude?" questioned Ann.

"It's been a while if you know what I mean, and I'm just letting off some steam. The projectile I fired at your boys was an electromagnetic pulse bomb that temporarily grounded their suits. It was a proximity explosion, that's why the others weren't affected."

"Interesting," said Ann. "We've had some recent solar mass ejections, we think on the same wave length as your weapon more than likely was. Now, back to why you're here, you got our attention as I assume you planned to do. And you want what from us?"

"I'd like a job," said the major, "that is, if you have room for one more genius and are done torturing me with bread and water. I could help you with the problem you're having with the shielding, too."

"I will consider your offer. In the mean time, these gentlemen will escort you to take a shower and get a change of clothes," she said.

"So, you're the man in charge. It's very nice to make your acquaintance," he said to Ann.

Two men in black security uniforms walked into the room and grabbed Holliday by his arms. He winked at Ann as he was taken out of the room.

"What do you think," Jim asked Steve as they watched the live feed from the control room.

"I've read his bio and think he would be a welcome asset to our ventures."

"I agree," said James, "but I think he may have been off the reservation too long. He's verbally abusive to everyone and very arrogant."

"He's always been that way," said Craig who had just entered the room. "He is however one of the smartest men I ever met in the intelligence community, or anywhere for that matter"

"Do you know him personally then?"

"I met him at the Pentagon during a joint exercise years back, when we were both just captains," said Craig. "He had the ability even then to make a very smart military man speechless."

"I don't know about giving him the gene therapy," said Doug. "He could be our greatest asset, or become our worst fear."

"I agree with you," said Jim, "but we have to at least try. This man is almost on our level without using all of his brain power. He could bring everything we don't know or understand into full swing."

"We don't know yet if he is even compatible right?" asked James.

"I just took a sample from him," said Ann. "We'll know soon enough."

Once the base was fully manned and the old airstrip was more or less gutted and abandoned, Gary and Trevor didn't have as much to do. There were less accidents and sickness and there were actually more medical personnel than patients. The population on the desert base was around four thousand at any given time. Some people found other ways to contribute and still others started new careers from what they did years prior. With the advanced intelligence that many now possessed, they could do almost anything, and did.

Ann and Simon's research into whose DNA was compatible with who resulted in the invention of a machine that, after receiving a live sample from each prospective partner, would issue them results within minutes. It was advised that anyone that wanted to procreate take the test. It would be safer for everyone, even if it was emotionally damaging. Some couples were found to be able to reproduce together and many others were not.

Chapter Fifteen: Completion

Once all the ships were completed, they would all go to the desert base in an area designated for final preparation and fitting. The ships all had their individual names, but once they were joined together the whole would be called Galaxias Exprimo or Galactic Explorer.

Construction would continue on more ships that would stay and help out on Earth. More cruisers were planned for quelling uprisings if any happened, protecting the planet, transporting people for work and supplies, for security, and as commuter ships in the future. With the advanced, clean energy that powered all current ships and would power future vessels, there would be no more need of fossil fuels for anything. The reliance on many natural resources was over and people could focus on living their lives and realizing their full potential.

True, clean energy was the plan. With no more government oversight or environmental organizations blocking progress or lawyers and courts bickering over who is right or wrong, it could all get done right and faster than ever.

The ion pulse generators that were currently powering all the communities would eventually be tied in together, an entire power grid on each continent as the populations grew and the communities were expanded into other areas.

It would take time to rebuild everything, but the remaining people on the planet were survivors. The efforts being made by individual communities would eventually bring prosperity to all.

Major Holliday's genome had been found compatible and he was being evaluated for inoculation.

James and Steve had asked to have Major Holliday brought into the R&D wing to show them how he built his weapon, the one that temporarily grounded Joe's and Tom's suits. There was still the issue with the solar flares and the different gamma rays detected recently. They had also disabled the suits and the ship. If they were the same, then they would hopefully be able to come up with a way around the problem.

Karen and a few other people were there as well. There was a viewing section in an upper room that had people in it too.

"You see," said Holliday, after looking at all the data and samples they offered him. "The reason your reflective shielding is absorbing the electromagnetic current temporarily is because you have the repulsion dialed up so high. If you lower it, the currents will just go around instead of being attracted. Who designed this technology?"

"I did," said Steve, "but I don't understand..."

"Well, that's the problem now isn't it? The material the suits and ships are made of will attract certain types of wavelengths. We need to make it so they are all deflected, not attracted," said the major.

"I understand the concept, that's not the problem," said Steve. "Why is the material only absorbing a certain current? That's where my confusion lies."

"You need to look at this from a sub-atomic level buddy. I'm going to guess that in your prior life that you were an engineer, am I right?"

"You are, but what does that have to do with anything? With the advanced intelligence we posse, this shouldn't even be an issue," said Steve.

"You were something else before you became what you are now," said Holliday. "You have all that you knew or thought you knew before holding you back, but that's who you are now too."

Steve just stared at him for a second and was about to speak before he was cut off again.

"I have proven my point yet again," said the major.

Steve was slightly frustrated, but focused and was able to turn the tides on the conversation.

"If we dial up the suits' current instead of diminishing it and emit our own electromagnetic field, then on your sub-atomic level we can actually harness the current that is effecting the material and use it as a weapon," said Steve.

"Yeah," said Holliday, "that would work too. We would have to design a core that could absorb and store the energy and design a weapon that could fire it back out."

The two men continued to bounce ideas off of each other while the others got back to work. They were all very impressed with Holliday. The major was scheduled to get inoculated the following day and was looking forward to it. He had been informed of the plans with the ships and had made his decision to stay on Earth to help rebuild the planet.

Chris's ship, the Paratus was almost done and could soon join the fleet. Preparations were made for the future mining facilities they needed for obtaining raw material. They were being designed in a pre-fabrication way so that they could be transported to any location, set up, and broken down with ease. The Virtus would be the only ship left on the planet until more ships could be built, once the others left. Construction and many other ventures would slow down while the transition happened. With the speed that the Virtus could travel, it would be able to shuttle people and supplies almost as fast as two ships could. The issue was the pilot. Others would need to be instructed on piloting the craft in order to give Steve a break from time to time.

There was enough scrap material to build at least one more ship and part of another stacked up by the smelting plant. They wasted no time in getting the material ready once enough was sent to the fabrication facility for use on the Paratus. Until told otherwise, crews would prep material for construction of more cruiser-class ships.

Once they had multiple ships to defend Earth, they would start work on commuter and mining ships too. Simulators were constructed and pilots in training were using them to learn how to fly the advanced crafts.

Chapter Sixteen: Hard Choices

The decision to leave or to stay was an easy one for some and tough for others. The calling to go forth and explore the cosmos was very strong for most. The Earth was their home, but some felt that the only way to restore life to its previous grandeur was to find the answers to life itself.

Karen had been somewhat standoffish for some time whenever Steve was around. He finally came out and asked her about it. "Is everything alright?"

"It couldn't be better," said Karen. "Why would you ask me that?"

"Just the way you've been acting," said Steve. "What have I done that I don't know about?"

"I'm not going with everyone else, and neither is your son, and our new baby isn't even here yet. I don't know why..."

"Why would you think we would be going with the rest of our friends?" asked Steve cutting her off mid sentence.

"I heard you talking with the men when you were walking down the ramp of the ship the other day," said

Karen. "You said you couldn't wait to get up there and explore."

"We were talking about Mars," said Steve with a smile. "After the Galactic Explorer takes off on its journey and we get back on track here, I mentioned that the rest of us that stay here should go and visit Mars. It's already given us a metal that we don't have on Earth and there could very well be more there to discover."

"I am so sorry," said Karen. "I should have asked you instead of just assuming. I've been feeling very emotional and tired."

"We need to go talk to Gary right away and make sure this is all normal with the pregnancy. Maybe you've been pushing yourself too hard," said Steve.

The two of them went off to go find Gary and hopefully get some good news. The whole population of the base had to make some decisions concerning the path that that they would take. None of the normal humans could go on the exploratory mission with the others. Without knowing how long the ship would be out there looking for habitable planets, searching for a place with gravity, they shouldn't go. The problems that humans can have after even a short time in zero gravity weren't worth the risk. Once new technology was introduced or a shorter flight time to a destination was available, they could go. One idea was being tested in simulations. It involved refreshing a sleeping body with blood continually, and sending electrical currents through all the muscles in the body to keep them stimulated. The people that altered their genome didn't need to do this.

They would probably have to sleep more so their body could repair itself more often, but they should theoretically be just fine even, for deep space travel.

Short trips to Mars would likely be okay for most people. If a future mining colony was established on the surface, regular humans would be assisting in the venture too.

Steve and Karen, along with a few others, made the decision to stay on Earth and continue with rebuilding humanity. With their knowledge and power, they could build a new and better civilization. Many more worthy humans would be chosen to help them transform the planet and set it on its new path.

The infrastructure for the new world model had been put in place when the so-called superhuman invincible people started putting up walls and re-establishing electric grids. The advanced technology they used didn't need constant maintenance. The small building surrounding the core, as it was called, was impenetrable. The short-lived resistance movement used many different weapons and explosives to try to get in, but nothing had worked. After the fall of the resistance, more people saw the people with the ships as a good and welcome thing.

Silvia and Rachael decided they wanted to stay on Earth. Chris and Kerri understood their decision, but still didn't like it. They all knew they would see each other again someday, but also knew it wouldn't be for a very long time. Their family had survived so much and being separated with such a great distance between them wouldn't be easy.

Gary and Nancy would stay on Earth too. They both wanted to continue helping the people of their planet. They were curious about what may be out beyond the solar system, but knew for now they belonged where they were. "Maybe someday," Gary told everyone.

Trevor wanted to go and explore. He wanted to bring his knowledge of medicine to other races should they encounter any. Simon felt like he had done as much as he could do on Earth. The plant and animal hybrids that he had helped with were flourishing in captivity and in the wild. He was very happy with their outcome. They would be able to continue to feed countless generations. Like Trevor, if he could take his knowledge and help others, he wanted to try. He would be taking all of his research and many samples with him not only for the crew, but for others he hoped to encounter.

For many others, the choice had been made years before. Exploration was what most of them lived for. If not exploring places, then things.

The Paratus was finished and the new facility constructed. The facility allowed them to test the ships once completed and fly them right out of the building. It was an exciting day and everyone that could be on hand to watch was there.

Chris put all the systems through pre-flight tests with his crew, and was ready for the test flight after getting the go ahead from the people on the ground. He had been flying with the different ship's commanders after going through simulations for a while and was ready.

"Tower, this is the Paratus requesting permission to depart the construction facility," said Chris.

"Roger that Paratus, you are all clear," said a suit soldier in the security tower after checking all the monitors.

Chris took the ship out of the facility slowly and moved out over the other buildings. He slowly rose in altitude, then in an instant, vanished before everyone that was watching.

"This is great," said Chris out loud to his crew.

The ship continued to gain altitude and flew through the atmosphere at a great speed. The ship went faster as Chris flew toward the moon. The maiden voyage of his ship would be one to the moon. Ever since he was a boy, he had looked up and wanted badly to walk on the lunar surface. In a few hours, he would be living one of his greatest dreams from the ship he commanded.

Not all of the crew members on board each ship had made up their minds about leaving the planet. There were plenty of other people in line to take their place if they chose not to go.

Samantha wanted to go, but Jake wasn't sure. He wanted to stay with her, but the thought of leaving and not knowing how it would go didn't sit very well with him. They had been through so much together and he didn't want to be apart, so he had a lot to think about.

Craig and Hans had made a pact to go and explore. They were both gunners on different ships, but would be on the same ship for the journey. Both men were alone and their camaraderie was the only thing either of them had left. Hans had been seeing Sara sometimes, the gunner from Jill's ship, the Fortis. They didn't have anything serious, but the two Marines would always be there for each other no matter what.

Some people stepped out of the way for others that really wanted to go on the exploratory mission. In the end, the majority of people were happy about their posts and how they could help out the collective.

Chapter Seventeen: Leaving

The ships were all completed and they fit perfectly together on the ground, making one massive intergalactic ship just as they were designed to do. Three ships folded in their stabilizing wings and connected together to form the rear and main thrusters for the whole. Two more made up the center and the last was the nose. Next, the ships would leave the base and enter a high orbit around Earth to make the massive ship fit together again and test it in space. The ships and their crews would soon be leaving for the closest planet in the habitable zone that might have an atmosphere and possibly life.

All the preparations that were needed for a long journey were put into place. Redundancy after redundancy was installed or added if it wasn't already there. Each ship was self sustainable, but when they were all attached, they would have each other's resources and crews to help out in every way. Most would be sleeping in a near comatose state while a small group would be awake taking care of all the systems and making sure everything went well on the journey. They would be traveling a great distance and didn't know when or if they would find other life among the stars. With most of the crew sleeping, not many resources would be used by the ones that were awake.

At the end of 2012, a planet was discovered closer to Earth using a telescope and a special instrument that allowed astronomers to pick up small gravitational wobbles of planets that were a certain distance from their parent star. The planet was named HD 40307g and was thought to be only about forty-two light years from earth. With the estimates that they had for now, the trip should just take about two years, maybe less.

This new information was found in the database that Steve had put together before the bombs fell in the old world. This would become the first destination for the Galactic Explorer. It was much closer than the original first stop on the list. All possibilities had to be investigated.

For now Kepler 22 b was the name of the second planet on their list of those to visit, and it was around 600 light years away. Even if life or a habitable atmosphere was found on HD 40307g, more planets had to be visited. All the information that Steve had in his servers about the Kelper Space Telescope, the exploratory spacecraft that was launched in 2009 to seek out these types of worlds, was downloaded onto each of the ships' data drives. There were hundreds of planets in conditions mimicking Earth's solar system that Kelper found during its galactic plane search, similar stars and planets orbiting those suns at the same distance that Earth sits to its sun. Kepler 22 b is in the Orion Spur of the Milky Way galaxy in the constellation Cygnus. The distance of 600 light years didn't sound very far to some of the travelers until they saw how many billions of miles it is on a theoretical map of what scientists think the galaxy looks like.

Once out of the solar system and beyond the ecliptic plane, the large ship would be able to go faster, because it would be out of the gravitational pull of the sun and planets. It was estimated that it would take about twenty years at the speed that the very large ship should be able to travel, but it could take less. With three of the ships' engines pushing the combined effort of the whole, the larger ship could fly at a very fast speed. They wouldn't know exactly how fast until they were all hooked together and the test flight to Neptune was under way.

The test flight was estimated to take a few months, but once maximum speed was reached, it would all become clear as to what the ship was capable of.

The asteroid belt between Mars and Jupiter has many voids in it and the asteroids could all be avoided as long as the trajectory was calculated correctly. Everything in the solar system was in an orbit around the sun and they all had to be put into the flight computer to maximize the flight time. As the large ship traveled out into the cosmos, everything would be tracked and picked up by the ships' sensors, then recorded as well. The flight data would be recorded on the ships themselves and streamed back to Earth for the others that stayed behind, so they could track where the ship went.

Beyond the solar system is an interstellar medium. The interstellar medium is the vacuum of space between different star systems, though this space is not entirely an empty vacuum. There is thought to be dust and other particles in it, in addition to cosmic rays and magnetic fields. The ship would be well protected from most things that may be encountered. Because of the vast expanse, the ship could hopefully navigate through any hazards, even flying at very fast speeds. Until they were out there and going through whatever is actually there, they considered it a guessing game.

"This is exciting isn't it?" Kerri asked Chris as they were packing all of the belongings they decided to take with them. Certain items wouldn't be good to take with them as they would be weightless for an extended period. If they really wanted to bring those items, they would have to be stored in containers until they found a place with gravity. They would hopefully find a planet with gravity and all the elements compatible for humans to live on, but a moon would be fine for awhile as they lived on the ship.

"This is a dream come true," said Chris. "I was hoping to be taking tour ships into orbit by this time, but to actually venture out past our solar system, I never thought it possible."

All ship commanders briefed their crews separately and then everyone got together for one final mission brief. There were ten crew members slotted for each ship. With Ann and Doug's son, there would be a total of sixty-one people going up on the exploratory mission. The round trip flight to Neptune would commence the following morning after the final preparations had been made. The ships would depart the base separately and then move into formation for integration once in a high orbit. Construction on the fabrication facility would be put on hold for a day so that they could all witness the launch of the Galactic Explorer on its test flight. The whole thing would be well documented and the video would be displayed for everyone to watch on all available monitors on the base.

The next morning, the base was alive earlier than normal as the ship crews got ready to leave and many others got up to watch history in the making.

The ships had been tested on the ground, hovering and moving into place, but this would be the first test in the vacuum of space. The time came and as soon as all crews were on board, Doug gave the command to all ships to launch and meet in orbit at the designated coordinates.

"This is crazy cool isn't it?" Billy said to Allie as the two, now more mature, teenaged kids sat on a couch in a lounge watching the large monitor.

"It's very exciting," said Allie. "I wish I could go with them."

"Yeah, me too, we've all come so far in such a short amount of time," he said, as he put his hand on Allies.

She thought about pulling her hand away, but looked over at Billy, who she knew liked her, and decided to just let him. She knew he was just trying to sound like he was smart, to impress her. The two teenagers sat there holding hands while they watched the satellite imagery of the ships connecting together.

The ships were all in orbit and maneuvering one at a time into position to attach to the others. Everything worked as planned as Doug guided all of them into their places while watching from outside cameras. As soon as a ship was close to docking, clamps would extend, lock and finish bringing the ships together.

"We have a hard seal Fortis," said Doug as the third ship was locked into its position.

"Roger that," said Jill.

As the rest of the ships got into their positions and locked in place, Doug calibrated the computers to obtain the best trajectory for the mission. He put the destination into the navigational computers and it calculated the most efficient course. The ship couldn't just fly in a straight path; it had to bound off the other planets to obtain greater speeds, a slingshot maneuver, used to reach the destination in the very large orbit around the sun. Voyager 1, a probe that was launched in 1977, took twelve years to reach Neptune. The ship they had now was much larger and their very modern technology was going to help it attain much greater speeds than the probe did. This test flight was going to give them the data they needed to figure out how long it would take to reach the other destinations they wanted to visit outside of the solar system.

After the destination was put into the navigational computer and all of the data was evaluated, the best course was to slingshot off of Mars and fly through the system toward Neptune. Once the ship got half the distance to the gas giant, the engines would be shut off and they should still be able to maintain that top velocity. Once they were three quarters of the way to the planet, they would have to slow down in order to establish an orbit and go over all the data collected.

With so many unknowns, they would have to wait and see if the current laws of known physics were correct.

"We're ready to go out," said Doug to everyone listening on the radio.

"From all that we can tell from here, you're good to go," replied Steve.

"Ship commanders, I have total control now. You can sit back and enjoy the ride," said Doug. He started all three engines and when they were all in sync, he slowly dialed the throttle up. Craig set all of the ion pulse cannons to auto to take care of any space junk that might happen to get in their path. The outer hull with the enhanced properties should protect them from any small bullet like pieces. It worked to stop anything thrown at it when Steve tested a suit.

The ship moved out of Earth's orbit and accelerated toward Mars for the slingshot. It picked up momentum slowly and as the minutes passed, the acceleration grew exponentially. In a few hours, they were almost half the distance to Mars and were not at full power yet. Doug wanted to slowly add more thrust in order to test all systems gradually. Within ten hours of leaving Earth's orbit, the Galactic Explorer was getting ready to kiss the atmosphere of Mars and perform the maneuver that would accelerate them even more. Once they were on the other side of the slingshot, they would be able to continue to accelerate the engines to maximum. They would be out of all contact for a short time while this happened. Steve and the others in the command and control center would wait until the ship contacted them.

Sometime later, intermittent static could be heard on the radio.

"It must be them," said Steve as the whole room got quiet.

"Control, can you hear us?" came a faint and garbled voice.

"We can hear you and we are picking up your signature again."

"We've made it through the slingshot and have accelerated well past the smallest moon of Mars. I will be accelerating the engines soon."

Doug's voice was becoming clearer as he talked. The beacon on the ship was showing their signature on the three dimensional model of the solar system as moving very fast. This was exciting news to many in the control room. The theories of so many scientists over the years were finally being put to the test. The ship continued to pick up speed and as it passed the asteroid belt between Mars and Jupiter, it maintained and didn't keep accelerating once the engines were shut down days later.

The ship would reach Neptune in a few weeks at its current speed. Once they established an orbit and were all satisfied with the data, they would move past the planet further out into the system and then turn around to use it to slingshot back to Earth.

Construction continued as much as possible with only one ship available to ferry people and supplies. The next ship wouldn't be completed for a few months, but once it was, the work tempo would increase as more material was mined and brought in.

Steve and Al Holliday were now working together in the research and development wing of the base. Karen was still working there, but not as much as she was pregnant and had De Novo and Postremo to care for when they weren't in daycare.

"I'm not a physicist or an expert on planetary science yet," said Al one day after spending some time on a computer, "but I think we need to build a beacon that the Explorer can pick up on a return flight down the road."

"What do you mean we should build a beacon?" asked Steve.

"From what I have figured out, the solar system and the galaxy are constantly moving according to the so-called experts in the database. If the ship is gone out of this system for even a short time, they might have a hard time finding their way home if this is correct."

"I see where you're coming from," said Steve. "Even with the sensors picking everything up as they leave the system and begin to compile data for star charts, unless they can account for stellar drift they would be useless."

"That is exactly what I just said, but using different words," retorted Holliday.

"Now boys, why does the testosterone always flare up when men are trying to figure something out?" asked Karen. "You're both intelligent and will figure it out together. There are no awards for finishing first anymore."

The guys got back to work on developing a long-range transmitter that could be encrypted and picked up only by their people. Al brought up the idea of installing one onboard the early warning satellite Steve had constructed, one of which was in orbit around Saturn along with another on Earth.

The Galactic Explorer reached Neptune in three and a half weeks. Once they established an orbit, the combined entire crew got to work analyzing all the data. Considering the speeds that they reached in conjunction with an ever-moving system, they were able to close the gap between great distances much easier. The mission would become a standard example for all future interstellar travel. The ship would soon be on the return trip to Earth and then getting ready to leave the solar system and explore.

Back on Earth, many people worked hard toward the final preparations and provisions for the long trip.

Even if the ship didn't find any life among the stars, they would be out there for a long time and would need as much food, air and water as they could carry.

Life on planet Earth would continue in their absence, and the current inhabitants would make sure that history didn't repeat itself.

"*I don't think the human race will survive the next thousand years, unless we spread into space.*"
—Stephen Hawking

About The Author

Travis Wright was born and raised in a small, Oregon town, where his love of the outdoors first began. He grew up hunting and fishing in the rural northwest, a lifestyle that transferred easily to a life in the last frontier. Wright has been in Alaska for 22 years, and now lives in Soldotna with his wife and five children—a daughter and four teenage boys.

When he's not busy with his family or trekking through backcountry, Wright works in the retail gun store he's owned and operated for 14 years. He is an NRA certified instructor and enjoys teaching others gun skill and safety.

Wright's interest in firearm technology as well as his active duty in the Marine Corps infantry are both influential in his work as a writer. While Wright has written poetry off and on for most of his adult life, his work as a novelist began in 2010 with the survival story Uncertain Times. Since putting that work to rest, he hasn't stopped writing. Wright's lifelong active imagination and curiosity have found their outlet in storytelling.

More ideas for stories are emerging all the time. Look for them to be published soon.